# Naughtier Bedtime Stories

**Books by Joan Elizabeth Lloyd**

THE PRICE OF PLEASURE

NEVER ENOUGH

CLUB FANTASY

NIGHT AFTER NIGHT

THE SECRET LIVES OF HOUSEWIVES

NAUGHTIER BEDTIME STORIES

# Naughtier Bedtime Stories

## JOAN ELIZABETH LLOYD

KENSINGTON BOOKS.

KENSINGTON BOOKS are published by

Kensington Publishing Corp.
850 Third Avenue
New York, NY 10022

ISBN-13: 978-0-7394-7745-8

Printed in the United States of America

# CONTENTS

# Introduction

I love a good erotic story and judging from your wonderfully positive reaction to *Naughty Bedtime Stories*, you do as well. So here are many more of my personal favorites. Combine a delicious short story with your own imagination and you can be anyone, do anything, with any partner and no one will be the wiser. Want to play with a shower massager? Want to join the mile-high club? Want to drink a love potion or feed one to the partner of your choice? Using the stories in this book you can do all of those things and so many more.

Read the tales here privately or gather your courage and share them with your lover. Read them silently, or aloud, alone or cuddled in bed with your partner. If a story here makes you smile or piques your sexual curiosity, don't keep that a secret. If you don't feel brave enough to read it to your lover, slip a bookmark in the page and put the book into your partner's briefcase or lunch box. He or she will certainly understand, and you'll both benefit from your bravery.

Erotica is highly personal and you might find that a story doesn't appeal. Just skip it and go on to the next. I know there will be many you'll want to read again and again.

So let's begin.

# The Cave
# of Delight

IT WAS SPOKEN OF around the village, but only in whispers. Bret had heard about the Cave of Delight from his older brothers, not as fact but as something young men fantasized about. No one would admit to having searched for it, but everyone knew that in the twilight boys from the surrounding area wandered through the woods and searched at the foot of the nearby mountains. No one had ever found it, at least not that anyone knew.

The Cave of Delight. All one's sexual fantasies came true inside. The most beautiful women would do anything to make you happy. But, according to the rumors, you could stay for only one night, after which you could never return. It would be a night worth whatever it cost, and Bret would pay any price.

So Bret searched. Every evening after working in his father's fields, he would take off in a different direction and walk until it got dark, then find his way home by the light of the lantern he carried. And occasionally he didn't return until morning. No one noticed, and he was completely at home out in the open.

One afternoon he finished his plowing, and, with a sack containing his lantern, a loaf of bread, and a small wheel of cheese, he took off in a new direction. Soon he would marry, he thought. The match had been arranged for him by his family, and he hadn't yet seen the woman. It didn't matter. Marriage was for bearing children—strong sons to work in the fields, beautiful daughters to help their mother and eventually marry into powerful families. Good loving? Bret sighed. He hoped so and would do whatever he could to make it so, but from what he knew of his married friends and brothers, it was usually rather ordinary. It would be comfortable sex every evening if he wanted.

As the shadows lengthened and the air cooled, he kept walking toward faraway hills. Suddenly he saw a rabbit disappear behind some rocks. Realizing that he'd never been aware of anything behind the small rockfall, he followed the rabbit. Finding a small passageway, he wiggled through the narrow opening and crawled through a low tunnel.

He heard water running and felt warm air on his face, and he kept crawling. Finally the tunnel sloped downward and widened. When the ceiling became high enough, Bret stood up and walked, ending up in a small cave. He looked around in the dim light, his eyes barely able to make out the rock walls and the small pool at the foot of a low waterfall. How could he see at all in a completely enclosed cave? Where was the faint illumination coming from? He shook his head and set his pack on a ledge.

He walked to the edge of the pool and dipped his fingers in the water. Rather than the cold of the springs near the farm, this water was almost hot. Again he looked around. Nothing but rock. He realized he was hot and sweaty and thought a dip in the warm spring would feel wonderful. He quickly stripped off his clothes and walked into the water. In the center, the water came up to his shoulders so he lifted his feet and floated on the smooth surface.

"I didn't think you'd be able to swim," a soft voice said.

Bret stood up and looked around the inside of the cave but saw no one. "Who's there?" Nothing. He must have imagined the voice, but it had sounded so clear. After a few moments, he lifted his feet and put his head back, lifting his hips to the surface.

"Very beautiful," she said.

Suddenly he realized that he was naked, and he stood so the water concealed his body. "Okay, stop fooling around. Who's there?"

Her laugh was musical, and he knew that he'd never heard anything like it before. "Me," she said.

Again Bret stood up. "And who's me?"

"You can call me Marie." There was a splash and he felt, rather than saw, a presence in the pool. Her head surfaced beside his, and he got a dim look at his companion. Although he couldn't see her very well, he knew that she was beautiful. He couldn't tell what color her long wet hair was nor could he see her eyes clearly, but her skin was like ivory, her neck long. She stood beside him, and she was almost as tall as he was.

"I just found this cave," Bret said, "but I guess you've known about it for a while."

"Oh yes. I come here often." She ducked beneath the warm water, and he felt her hair brush against his flank as she swam below the surface. He reached down and grabbed at her and felt bare, soft flesh. Her buttocks? Was she as naked as he was?

She surfaced, and her musical laugh filled the cave. "So, you want to play." Again she dove, and he felt hands on his thigh. Shaking his head, he, too, dove beneath the water and reached for anything he could touch. Her body was indeed naked, and his hands found her breasts and her ankles.

For long minutes, they dove, surfaced, laughed, and dove

again, until Bret was breathless. Finally the two stood side by side in the water, panting. "You are very handsome," she said when she could breathe easily again.

"And you are very beautiful," he said.

Then her lips were against his, and the length of her lush body pressed his. Her hand cupped his head as the kiss lengthened. This wasn't play anymore, and his body knew it. He was hard and her hand found him, circling his erection with long fingers.

When he groaned, she laughed, her joy obvious. "Wonderful," she said, holding him under the warm water. She cupped his balls and touched the tender spot just in front of his anus. He reached for her and held her breasts, stroking the soft skin, teasing her hard nipples.

"You must stop," he said.

"But why?" she asked.

"You don't know what will happen if you continue."

"Of course I do, silly. And it will be magnificent. I know." She continued to knead his hardness, forcing him to concentrate on not spurting yet. This was too fantastic. Her hands felt so good touching him, and her breasts filled his hands. He slid his palms around to her back, then down to cup her buttocks. He lifted her, and she wrapped her thighs around his waist.

He pushed her upward and, as her head fell backward, took one turgid nipple in his mouth. He suckled, listening to her moans of pleasure, trying to extend their tender lovemaking. But he knew his body would wait no longer. He lowered her slowly along the length of his chest and was inside her with one smooth thrust, the water cushioning his movements. In perfect rhythm they matched their motions as his erection slid in and out of her slick passage. It was going to be too quick, he knew, as he felt his orgasm boiling in his belly. His fingers found her clit and he rubbed, trying to increase her obvious pleasure.

"Oh yes," she screamed, and he felt small spasms ripple through her channel. His back arched, and too soon he erupted deep inside of her.

He didn't make it home that night. They stayed together in the cave, sharing his bread and cheese and making love many more times. Finally she told him that he would have to leave. "I don't want to go," he moaned.

"I know, but you have to. You are allowed only one night."

"This is the Cave of Delight?" he gasped.

"I thought you knew," she said.

He was desolate. But he knew where the opening of the cave was, so he could find it again. He would. "I hadn't thought about it, but I want to return."

"I know, but it is impossible."

Slowly he put his clothes back on, determined to come back that very night. He kissed her good-bye, and, as he crawled back through the tunnel, he heard her magical laugh.

He returned to the rocks that night, but there was no opening, no tunnel, no cave. Night after night he combed the rocks but, alas, no cave.

Months later, he was resigned to his marriage. Maybe she'd be more than he expected, yet she could never be Marie. Never.

Two days before his wedding, he traveled to his future wife's village with his parents and his eldest brother. When they arrived at her family's farm, he was seated in the small main room, and he watched as she slowly glided down the stairs. She was quite lovely, with long auburn hair and soft, white skin. "My name is Jane," she said, "but my friends call me by my middle name, Marie."

"Marie?" he said, pained by the coincidence.

"Yes," she said, lowering her eyes. "You can call me Jane if you prefer."

He had to forget the night in the cave. It was a fantasy, and this was reality. "Of course I will call you Marie."

"And you are Bret. I like that name."

They talked for a few minutes, then were called into the dining room for dinner. She went into the kitchen to help with the serving, and suddenly he heard her musical laugh. It was her laugh, the angel from the cave. She walked from the kitchen, still laughing. It was her. There could be no mistake. As she sat beside him, he whispered, "It was you, wasn't it?"

"It was the cave of your delight, what you wanted most. Many have been there, and each gets what he most desires. You wanted a lover and a wife in one."

"But how?"

"I do not know, and you must not reveal any of what happened or it will disappear. Just be content that we can have our desires for the rest of our lives."

Bret couldn't control his grin. He was the happiest and luckiest of men.

# The Model

JUSTIN LAY stretched out on his bed with the most recent copy of the Geneva Toy Company catalog propped on his stomach. He stared at the model clothed only in a sheer stretchy black cat suit with a pattern of vines, roses, and leaves woven in. Her well-developed breasts were clearly defined beneath the lacy fabric. He sighed and traced her outline with his index finger. "I'd really love to play with that," he whispered.

"And so you shall," a woman's voice sighed into his ear.

"Yeah, right," he growled. "Now I'm hearing voices."

"No, you aren't. You're hearing me."

Justin sat up and looked around. There was nothing out of the ordinary in his room. "Hearing who?" he asked. "Where the hell are you?"

"Right here," the voice said, seeming to come from the foot of his bed.

"Right where?"

"Here."

Justin stared at the place from which the voice seemed to be coming. The air appeared to shimmer, like when you drive down a road in the summer and you see the heat rising off the pavement. The air became somehow less transparent, as though seeing his dresser through a gauzy curtain. "What the fuck's going on here?"

"Just be patient. You have to be patient."

The air thickened, and slowly a shape began to appear. There was a torso, then legs. Long, shapely legs that seemed to rise forever from a pair of black, high-heeled shoes. The torso solidified, and soft breasts, a flat belly, and narrow hips were visible. Shoulders appeared, with long arms, then hands with long fingernails polished bright red. A head formed from a small plume of hazy smoke, the face smiling, the hair wild and black. As she became a woman, he realized that she was indeed the model from the catalog, dressed in the lacy, black cat suit in the picture.

"Just a few moments more," she said as her body thickened and became three dimensional. "It takes less and less time each time I do this."

"Excuse me?"

"I've learned to materialize when a man wishes for me. And you did."

"I did?" Justin was totally bemused. What was happening? Was he losing his mind? This kind of thing just didn't happen. Not to sane men. He raked his fingers through his shoulder-length brown hair.

"Yes. You said, and I quote, 'I'd like to play with that.' End quote. I distinctly heard you. *So*, here I am so you can play."

"Play?"

"Listen, buster, stop asking silly questions. You sound like the village idiot. And I've known my share, believe me."

Justin took a deep breath. "Okay. I'll stop asking questions if you explain what's going on."

"I told you," she said, sounding totally exasperated, "but I'll explain it one more time. You wished for me. I materialized. Sort of like the genie in the lamp, except you rubbed my body. Now I'm yours to play with. Do what you want with." She reached over and grabbed Justin's cock through the crotch of his jeans. "And I'll bet I know just what you want."

Justin almost said "Do anything?" but he thought one more question might make her disappear again. He looked her over carefully from head to foot, and he had to agree that he wanted to play with that. She was a perfect sex object, and the cat suit brought out both her best features. And great features they were. He reached out and touched the tip of one breast with the end of his index finger. His finger met warm, firm flesh.

Her laugh was deep and throaty. "No, your hand doesn't pass right through me. I'm real. Flesh and blood." She stepped back and placed her hands on her hips. "And not bad flesh it is, too." She turned left and right, modeling, showing off her fantastic body.

"Not bad at all," Justin said. "And it's really mine to play with?"

"All yours. What would you like?"

Oh God, he thought, what would he like? Everything. In his twenty-eight years, he'd never had an offer like that. Everything. Where to start? "How long do I have you for?"

"For now. The rest kind of works itself out." She cupped her breasts through the lacy black material of the cat suit. "Want to start here?"

"Oh yes," Justin said and cupped both palms over her magnificent breasts. He felt the nipples come alive in his hands as his fingers kneaded and squeezed. "Not too hard," she said. "Wouldn't want to bruise the merchandise."

"Sorry," Justin said. "Why don't you come here and sit beside me?"

She sat on the edge of the bed and, as Justin's hand continued to caress her breasts, unbuttoned his shirt. "Umm," she purred. "Nice. I'm not overly fond of big hairy chests. Yours is smooth and so good to touch." She ran her hands over his skin, touching all the places Justin loved to be touched. Her fingers were almost electric, causing shivers down his back. "Maybe you'd like me to take this off," she said, pulling at his shirt. He moved so his arms pulled out of the sleeves. "Yes," she purred. "Nice."

"And maybe you'd like to take that outfit off, too."

"Oh no." She fiddled with the front of the garment and soon two of the intricate leaves that had appeared to grow from the vines on the suit were in her hand. "These seem to be part of the pattern, but they really come off. See?"

He did see. The leaves that she had removed exposed her large deep brown nipples. "Very convenient." He pinched her swollen tips, causing them to get harder and tighter. "Very convenient."

She tugged at Justin's belt. "I thought you'd think so. It's for sale, but more of that later. How about taking this off?" she purred.

Justin needed no urging. His cock was so swollen that his pants had become terribly uncomfortable. What the hell? He stood, quickly pulled off his jeans and shorts. Now naked, he sat back down on the bed, his cock sticking straight up from his groin like a flagpole. "That's so big," she purred. "Can I touch it?"

Justin was afraid that if she touched his cock, he'd go off right then. What the hell? "Sure. Touch away."

She seemed to know exactly what he wanted. She wrapped her hand around his stiff cock and pushed down, then rubbed the tightened skin over the tip with the fingers of her other hand. She trapped the head of his cock in her hand, pressed down, and, as the head pushed through her tightened fingers, her other hand grasped it. Justin was in heaven.

"This would work better with some Geneva Lube," she said, and almost instantly a tube of slippery stuff appeared in her hand. She squeezed a big glob in her palm and went back to work, rubbing his cock. He was trembling with the excitement of it all, but he wasn't quite to the point of coming. It was as though she knew how to keep him just below his peak.

"Would you like me to lick it?" she asked, her voice soft and sensuous.

"Oh God," Justin groaned, dropping onto his back and spreading his legs.

"How about some Geneva-flavored gel?" she said and, as if by magic, a jar had appeared and she was spreading some on his cock. The scent of chocolate filled his nostrils. "It comes in strawberry and banana, too."

She sounded kind of like a commercial, but when her mouth enveloped his penis, he forgot everything else. Her mouth was amazing, as talented on his cock as her hand had been. She lay the flat of her tongue against the underside of his cock, then pulled her head back with just enough suction. Her tongue flicked the tip and swirled around the head. God, she was good. It felt as if he were soaring.

"Are you ready to fuck me?" she said a while later.

"Absolutely." If her pussy was as great as her hands and mouth, he was in for the best fuck of his life.

"A Geneva tickler," she said, unrolling a condom over his cock. "See," she added, "it has a little thingie on the end that unrolls when you come inside of me. Actually, I've never felt anything, but it's supposed to be the best so I always use one."

Before he had time to react, she straddled his hips and

lowered her hot pussy onto his cock. "See how convenient," she said. "The suit has no crotch so I can do this very easily."

Her hot pussy surrounded his cock, and she raised and lowered her body, fucking him expertly. "Good?"

"Oh God," he groaned, trying not to come. Make it last, he vowed, but it was no use. He climaxed almost immediately.

"That was really good," she said only moments later. "I have some Geneva towelettes here." She pulled off the condom and used the cool towel to clean his cock and balls. "See? All nice and clean. These are really useful for those away-from-the-bedroom fucks."

"Yeah," Justin moaned. "Convenient."

"Okay. How many would you like?"

"Huh?" Justin's fuzzy mind tried to understand what she was saying.

"How many? Or would you like a dozen of the tickler condoms. They're on sale this week."

"Okay, I'm gone. What's going on?"

"I was just trying to take your order."

"Order?"

"Sure. The cat suit's only forty-nine ninety-five. Or you might want to order the lube or the gel."

"But I don't want to order anything."

"So why were you looking at the catalog?" she asked, a bit bemused.

"I just like to look at your picture. And all the other girls, too."

"You don't want to order anything?"

"No. Not really."

"Nothing?"

"Nothing."

"Well then, it's been fun."

Slowly her body began to dissolve. "Wait," Justin said. "I don't get it."

"If you don't buy anything, you don't get the ordering service," she said. "Bye."

"But wait—"

"No order, no service. Sorry." And she was gone.

Justin stared at the spot where she had been, then picked up the catalog and gazed. Then he stroked the model's picture. "I'd really like to play with that," he said. But she never reappeared.

# The Monica Thing

HALLOWEEN had never been one of her favorite holidays, but as Linda surveyed the swirling mass of humanity, she realized that this party was going to be a real bummer. Halloween. Almost as commercial now as Christmas. People in her neighborhood had hung orange lights around their windows, for God's sake. This whole thing was crazy.

She had taken out her frustration with the holiday on her costume. Monica. Blue dress and black wig with a jaunty black beret set at a rakish angle. And a rubber mask that covered her face down to the mouth. She looked down. The dress even had a small stain in what she assumed was the right place. What a joke.

And this party. Too loud, too frantic, too . . . well just too. But she had promised her friend Val that she would attend, so attend she would. She had said her good evenings to Val, and hopefully, without too much notice, she'd slip out again after as short a time as possible, go home, and watch TV.

"Would you do it?" a voice said in her ear. She spun to see a Bill Clinton just behind her. He wore a well-tailored blue suit, wing tip shoes, and a rubber mask that covered most of his face. He was tall, his body lean, but she could make out little more than that and the fact that his eyes were brown.

"I'm sorry. Would I do what?"

"Give Bill Clinton head."

"Not a chance. I'm a devout Republican. I'd probably bite it off."

"I wouldn't like that," the man said, putting his hand on her arm, "but judging from the gorgeous sexy mouth of yours, you'd be great doing the Monica thing."

"Would you let me?"

"Okay, now I'm confused."

"Would you let someone you didn't know get her teeth that close to your prized possession?"

His laughter was spontaneous and genuine. "I don't suppose I would. But then in a few minutes we wouldn't be strangers, would we?" He smiled down at her. "Drink?"

A few moments ago she'd been planning her escape, but now she nodded. "I'd love a white wine."

"A Monica drink if there ever was one." He turned toward the bar. "Don't disappear."

"Would Monica do that to Bill?" Linda answered.

And she waited, amazed and exhilarated. She had no clue what the guy looked like or what kind of a person he was, but somehow she liked him. And he had sexy hands. She caught herself up short. Where had that thought come from? *Well, I'm just being honest. He does have great hands.* She had noticed his long, nicely shaped fingers as he had briefly held her arm. She was a sucker for sexy hands.

And that hand now held out a glass of white wine. "Let's go out onto the terrace," he said. "It's much quieter there, and maybe we can talk. Discuss politics, my being a Democrat and all."

Although it was the last night of October, the air was just warm enough to relax outside without getting chilled. They stood and talked for a while as they sipped their drinks. The talk never got personal enough for them to learn much about each other, but they laughed a lot and Linda felt charmed and completely comfortable. As she leaned on the railing, she shivered a bit.

"Chilly?" Bill asked, moving behind her. He wrapped his arms around her, his hands just beneath her breasts. "I have a great idea about how to warm you up, Monica."

This was moving much too fast, Linda thought, but his arms felt so good. His thumbs began to rub the undersides of her breasts, and she felt her body responding. This is nuts, she told herself. I don't know this guy's name or even what he looks like beneath that mask. Yet, I'm letting him touch me, and I'm enjoying it. Her Monica dress buttoned up the front, and she felt his fingers undo the buttons then his warm, sexy hands slip inside. As his fingers cupped her breasts, she allowed her head to fall back against his shoulder.

She didn't realize just how quickly things were moving until he flipped open the clasp at the front of her bra, and suddenly his hands were on her bare breasts. Her breasts, and particularly her nipples, had always been her downfall. Several of her ex-boyfriends had discovered that and taken advantage of her weakness, touching, biting, pinching until she was moaning, and willingly accepted anything they wanted to do with her.

His fingers were pinching her nipples, making heat lance down her body to her groin. She felt herself opening, moistening, readying herself for him. Oh God, she couldn't help responding to him.

And what would be the harm. He didn't have a clue who she was, and she didn't know him. A quick fling, then anonymity. What's the problem? She mentally shook her head. No problem.

Her back was still against his chest, and her buttocks detected how excited he was becoming as well. Hard, fully erect male flesh, only thinly covered by his Bill Clinton suit pants pressed into her cheeks. A soft moan escaped her lips. She was still looking over the city when one of his hands slid down and grabbed the front of her skirt. Slowly he lifted and pulled until his hand could grasp the front of her panties and slip inside. With one of his hands still kneading her breast and one rubbing her mound, she moaned. "Oh yes," he whispered. "Yes. So wet." He seemed to know just where to rub, touch, invade, and she tipped her pelvis so his fingers could slide into her channel. She wanted. Now!

She reached down and grabbed his hand, pressing the heel into her clit. She rubbed her body against his hand and arm like a cat in heat, until, with a small cry, she came. God, waves of pure pleasure rocked her. She grasped his wrist so tightly she wondered whether she would cut off the circulation. But she didn't care. She just needed.

It was long moments until the spasms subsided. "Oh God, baby," he moaned in her ear. "So incredibly responsive. I've never met anyone like you."

Linda caught her breath, then turned. "You asked me a question a while ago. I said I was a Republican." Her hands went to his zipper, and she slowly lowered it, feeling the huge mass of hardened cock beneath. "Would you trust a Republican?" As she worked his cock free of his clothing, she glanced around. Thankfully the terrace was empty. She slipped to her knees and wrapped her hand around the base of his turgid member. Knowing she wasn't able to take too much of him she wrapped her hand around the base of his hard prick, made an O with her mouth, and slowly sucked him inside. She had too active a gag reflex to do a deep throat, but her hand worked its magic. As she sucked on the end of his cock, she worked her hand rhythmically, squeezing her fingers in a pattern from her index finger on the base to her pinky about halfway up the shaft.

She knew he was close so she worked one finger in through his fly and rubbed his balls. He came with a loud groan, semen filling her mouth and making a fresh stain on her blue Monica dress.

She stood up and watched as he struggled to get his breath. What had she done? This was unthinkable. She wouldn't have dreamed of doing anything like this except for the costume. It was a Monica thing. Suddenly she was so embarrassed she wanted to slip into the house and disappear. She wasn't like this. She wasn't.

"Can I get you another glass of wine?" he asked.

"Thanks," she managed to say.

He walked into the living room, and quickly Linda slipped in behind him. She worked her way to the bedroom, grabbed her coat, and rushed out the front door. Almost running down the stairs, she pulled off her mask. What kind of a slut does he think I am? It doesn't matter, she told herself. He doesn't know who I am. She sighed. And it's really too bad. We made each other laugh a lot. Under other circumstances . . .

She tossed and turned all night, and, by eight the next morning, thankfully a Sunday, she was up, dressed, and sitting in her tiny kitchen, cradling a cup of coffee in her hands. When the phone rang just after nine, she slowly picked it up. "Hello?"

"Don't hang up, Monica, and don't be upset." He spoke quickly, getting the words out before she could think. "It's Bill. Last evening was wonderful, but much too fast. I didn't mean to behave like that, but I guess I just got carried away. Maybe if we had a regular date, without masks, we could begin again. Think about it. Please."

It was all Linda could do not to drop the phone. She

cleared her throat as all that had happened rushed through her mind, heating her body. She whispered, "Last evening should be forgotten."

"Last evening should be remembered and savored. It was sensational. And my name's Greg."

Linda hesitated. "How did you get my number?"

"I hounded Val until she gave it to me. She wouldn't give me your name and made me promise that I would forget the number if you weren't interested. Please. Give us a chance."

Linda couldn't help it. It was impossible not to smile. He was so sweet, and it had been so wonderful. "Okay," she said. "Hi, Greg. My name's Linda."

# The Perfect Mate

THERE WAS ONCE a princess named Tamara who had bullied her father into agreeing that she wouldn't have to marry anyone who wasn't her perfect mate. Over the past two years she had met and rejected seventeen princes, twenty-two noblemen, two sheiks from faraway kingdoms, and even several commoners. No one was handsome enough, tall enough, wise enough, witty enough. No one was good enough for Tamara, and she didn't even give them any time to impress her. No one was her perfect mate, and her father, the king, lamented that she might never marry.

One afternoon Tamara was practicing her serve on the royal tennis court, dressed in rags. She was a very good tennis player, but she wasn't sure just how good she really was because the members of the court always let her win. "Please," she would beg, "play your hardest. I need that."

"But your majesty . . ."

So today she was dressed as a scullery maid, stealing time from her job in the kitchen. "Aren't you worried about being caught?" a voice said.

"Caught?" she asked, gazing at the stranger. He was just her height, with thick glasses, a slightly balding head, and travel-worn clothes.

"Yes. Taking time from your duties in the kitchen must be a punishable offense."

"Oh. Yes. Well, I have a few minutes. Do you play?"

"A bit," the stranger said. "But I don't think I can play here. Isn't it for royalty only?"

"I'm playing here," Tamara said. "My name's Tammy."

"Hi Tammy. I'm Kurt." They shook hands, and he continued, "I'm a stable hand, new to the court. I'd love to play, but I've no racket."

Tamara got him a racket from the collection beside the court, then proceeded to be humiliated by his powerful serve and stinging backhand. Although her feelings were hurt, she couldn't help but admire his skill. As they walked to the side of the court, sweating and panting, he winked at her. "Good game."

Winded, she winked back. "Yes, a great game. Thanks."

"I particularly liked looking at your legs when you served."

Slightly flustered, Tamara blushed. "Thank you, but you're very forward."

"Not as forward as I'd like to be," he said, a wide grin splitting his face.

Tamara had never come anywhere close to the heady feeling of flirting with a stranger who knew nothing about her. "What would you do then, sir?"

"I'd tell you how beautiful your breasts look through that blouse. I couldn't help but watch them jiggle, and it almost cost me several points."

Blushing furiously, Tamara said, "You say the most outrageous things."

"And do the most outrageous things, too," he said. Then he placed his hands on her waist and pulled her against him. Slowly his lips descended until she could feel his warm breath on her mouth. He's going to kiss me, she realized, and I'm looking forward to it.

And he did. His mouth covered hers, softly at first, then more fiercely as he adjusted the kiss to take full pleasure in her mouth. As he held her more tightly, she felt her knees weaken and her heart pound. Her rapid breathing had nothing to do with their recent exercise. She realized that her hands were pressed against his heaving chest, and she slowly slid her palms up his shirt to cup the back of his head. As she threaded her fingers through his hair, she felt his grip tighten still more and his knee press against her legs.

Without even being aware, she parted her thighs and allowed his thigh to press between them. Finally, long moments later, Kurt leaned back. "You certainly know how to kiss," he said. "Why don't we meet later in the stable and continue this in private?"

Could she? Should she? Absolutely not! "Yes," she sighed. "An hour after dinner."

Was she crazy? she wondered as she finished her evening meal. She wouldn't let him take real liberties, but she had enjoyed his kiss and wanted . . . Wanted what? She didn't really know, but she needed to find out. Although she changed her mind several times, an hour after the meal ended she found herself in the stables.

The large room was lit only by a single lantern at the far end and was redolent with the smells of hay, horse, and leather. "I didn't think you'd come," his voice said from behind her.

"I didn't think so either," she answered honestly.

Then he was against her, pressing his chest to her back, his arms around her waist, his lips nibbling at the back of her neck. "Mmm," he purred, the vibrations transmitting to her very bones.

His hands wandered to her breasts, cupping her, squeezing her, and she felt her knees tremble and her private area getting wet. When he lightly pinched one nipple, she almost passed out from the pleasure of it. "Oh gracious," she gasped.

His lips roamed her neck and shoulders, and his hands kneaded her flesh until she felt a bubble growing in her belly. Then one hand traveled down her abdomen until he found her mound. He rubbed, pressing her spine against his belly. She reveled in the feel of his hand and his obvious hardness against her buttocks. She tried to keep still and just feel, but she couldn't keep her hips from rubbing against him.

"Oh, you wanton wench," he groaned, moving them into the darker recesses of one of the stalls. "You're such a sexy thing." His fingers pressed her skirt against her groin, and he rubbed, finding her hard clit. The sensations were muffled through the layers of fabric, but she moved so the rubbing was in the exact right spot.

"Oh," she moaned. "Oh." Something grew inside of her, coloring the dim room in bright oranges and blues, swirling before her closed eyes. As his talented fingers delved more deeply between her legs, colors exploded, wild blasts of bright reds and yellows, flying outward like fireworks. Her knees collapsed, yet his hands held her up, her back pressed against his chest.

"You're amazing," he whispered. He turned her around. "Now help me." He loosened his britches and released his erection.

Tamara had seen animals, but never a man. But he was magnificent, even in the very weak light. He guided her hand to him, and, hesitantly she touched him. Hard, yet like the smoothest, softest fabric. Warm, with a small drop of fluid oozing from the tip. "How?" she whispered.

He showed her, wrapped her fingers around him and covered her hand with his. Then he rubbed her hand along the length of his hardness, pressing the tips of her fingers into his flesh. "Faster," he groaned. "Yes. Like that."

In only a moment she felt his hips buck and suddenly thick, milky liquid spurted from the end of his prick. "Oh, God," he grunted, panting. "Magnificent."

For a long time they stood, leaning against the wall of the stall. "Tammy, I must see you again."

"And I need you, too," she said.

They cleaned up, then, hand in hand, they walked to the more brightly lit end of the stable. "You look familiar," Kurt said. "And your clothes." He looked her over. "You're not a kitchen worker, are you?"

"Well . . ."

"Oh shit . . . I know who you are. I saw you from a distance when I first got here. You're the princess."

"Yes. That's true."

"But then there's no future for us," he lamented.

"That's not necessarily true. Not true at all. Actually, I'd like to get to know you better. You just might be perfect."

# Blind Passion

IT WAS PITCH BLACK in her room as Maria was jarred awake by the feeling of hands on her wrists. Efficiently someone tied her arms to the headboard of the bed, and quickly a blindfold was secured over her eyes. As her panic increased, a soft hand stroked her forehead. "Do not be alarmed. I understand that this all feels very scary, but I want only pleasure for you."

Maria tried to concentrate on the calm, soothing voice, but despite the reassurances, her heart pounded and her breathing accelerated. The hand was so relaxing, gently caressing her temples and then her cheeks, but her arms couldn't move and she couldn't see. "Wh-what do you want?" she managed to say, her voice squeaky and quavering.

"Only your pleasure, as I told you. Please, try to relax. I assure you that it will be wonderful."

She tried not to cry. "Why have you assaulted me like this?"

"Assaulted? No. Never. We have our reasons for needing you like this. I want to say that you should trust me, but I know you cannot."

"Trust you?" Maria almost shrieked. "Trust you?" Her

laugh was almost hysterical, yet the hand on her face continued to soothe.

"I know," the man said. "I understand. It will take some time for you to accept that I mean you no harm."

Maria tried to quell the panic inside her. She was bound and blindfolded . . . yet comforted somehow. It made no sense. She felt the covers pulled off the bed, and she realized that the man could see her body through the short baby-doll pajama top she wore. "You are truly lovely," the man said. "It will be a pleasure to make you come alive."

"Come alive?" What the hell did that mean?

"Just try to relax as I said. You will soon understand everything."

What was there to understand? She was helpless, incapable of resisting anything he wanted to do to her. The hand stroking her face was so soft, caressing, but she couldn't succumb. She couldn't allow herself to relax and be raped. That was surely what was going to happen. Rape. By some unknown, unseen stranger.

Maria had always had rape fantasies, but this wasn't a fantasy, this was a real, disgusting assault. Yet the hand was so soft and was joined by a second one, touching her fingers and her palms as they were held incapable of moving in their bindings.

"I am so sorry it has to be like this," he said. "I know it is so frightening." He sighed, and somehow Maria almost felt sorry for him.

"Why are you doing this?" she asked. "You say you're sorry that it has to be like this, so don't do it."

"I am afraid it has to be," he said, his voice sounding almost sad. "But in the end, you will see how wonderful it will be."

Then Maria felt a soft kiss on her forehead, gentle, feather-soft like a mother's good-night kiss. The hands and the mouth combined to make her feel treasured, cosseted. As the lips neared her mouth, she almost parted her lips to receive the loving kiss. But she couldn't. This was so horrible.

Yet it wasn't really. How could she be of two minds like this, her brain screamed. You're being raped, yet somehow she felt that it was an act of love. "Just enjoy it," he said. "You have no choice, after all, so you might as well."

He had a point. Since she had no choices, why not just roll with things and see what happened? She should try to gather data for the police. She couldn't see anything, but what did she hear, or smell. She could stop fighting the inevitable and just go with it. She relaxed the muscles in her arms. Yes, she wouldn't fight, just gather information.

"Oh yes," he said, "that is so much better."

Learn. "Do you have a name?" Did he have an accent of some kind? That would be helpful.

"You can call me Joe." There were faint rustling sounds, and she felt him settle onto the bed beside her. "I would like to kiss you, but only when you are ready." He stroked a finger over her closed lips.

She felt her mouth open, almost of its own volition, and his finger touched her teeth. No one in her sexual past had ever been so tender, so loving. She'd been with lots of men, after all. She was almost twenty-five. But this was a first. Too bad she couldn't give in to it all. Could she? No. She was just finding out all the information she could. Right? Lips brushed hers, tentative yet sensual. She let out a long, low sigh, slowly flowing into the embrace. And it was better than any kiss she had ever had. This guy's a great kisser, she thought as her mind fuzzed. His tongue tentatively touched hers, tasting and learning what pleased her. Giving. She could no more help returning the magical kiss than she could stop breathing. She angled her head to better taste him in return, and his gentle hands cupped her face then tangled in her hair.

On and on. The kiss continued and quickly became her whole world. Was this wrong? It couldn't be. Not something so beautiful. The mouth began to wander, to her neck, her ears, her shoulders. He licked and caressed her throat and the tender hollow at the base. He slid his tongue down the pulse in her neck, and Maria felt it quicken, not in fear but in erotic enjoyment.

"Oh," she moaned, unable to control the feelings of pleasure as Joe's mouth found all the places that made her want. His mouth kissed its way down her breastbone as his hands caressed her sides. She heard a ripping sound, then her pajamas were gone.

"So lovely," Joe said.

She wasn't, and she knew it. She was almost thirty pounds overweight and was so afraid of the sun that she was pasty white all over. She knew that her saggy breasts were large, and that's what usually attracted the men she dated, and slowly, as they got to know her, not only did they want her body, but they genuinely liked her. But beautiful? Not!

A finger pressed against her lips. "A woman enjoying passion is always beautiful, so do not argue."

She sighed and swallowed the words she had been about to utter.

"Your breasts are soft and so white. They almost glow in the moonlight."

Moonlight. Joe had obviously opened the drapes. She had wondered why no light came through the fabric of the blindfold, and now she understood. The room was lit only by the moon.

Soft hands stroked the soft flesh at the sides of her breasts, swirling toward her now-erect nipples, yet not touching them. She heard a groan and realized that the sound had come from deep within her. Please, she screamed in her mind. Oh God, please. But she couldn't say it aloud. She couldn't admit that some rapist was giving her more pleasure than she had ever experienced before.

Then there was a mouth on her left breast, suckling at her nipple. Shards of ecstasy knifed through her, shooting from her breast to the hidden world between her legs. She felt her nether lips swell and moisten, opening for her lover. Lover? Her rapist. The rapist she wanted so desperately now.

Suddenly there was a mouth on her other breast. A second set of talented lips nursed and pulled at her nipple. There were two men. "No," she cried. "It's obscene."

The mouths continued, heedless of her protests. "No." And yet it became more and more difficult to object, the pleasure was so great.

"Yes, accept," Joe said.

But there were still two mouths suckling at her breasts so there had to be three men. Three? She couldn't think. This was some kind of gang rape. Yet . . .

Then there were hands. How many? She couldn't count and didn't care. Fingers tweaked her nipples, causing almost pain that further excited her. A mouth sucked on her toe. One nipped at the tip of her thumb. Fingers stroked the insides of her thighs, the backs of her knees, the insides of her elbows.

So many sensations she couldn't sort them out. She didn't have to. The erotic totality was richer than anything she had ever imagined. Then there were fingers stroking the deep valleys of her sopping pussy, exploring, arousing, massaging. She was flying, higher than she ever remembered. Whatever was happening, she could now focus only on her approaching climax.

A mouth found her swollen clit and sucked as a finger

slowly entered her. And as the finger invaded her pussy, one slid into her mouth. The two fingers adopted the same rhythm, fucking her in two places at once, while a mouth sucked on her clit and one suckled at each breast.

It was too much, and she came. Hard and long, spasms rocked her, tightening every muscle in her body. As she came, there was a sound like heavy moaning from the men in the room, a deep moan that she could almost feel through her body. It was so intense and lasting, it was several minutes before she could think. Were they going to fuck her now? Did she want that? "Oh my God," she moaned.

Now she could hear deep breathing in the room. She slowly became aware of the fact that her blindfold had loosened during her writhing and now permitted her to peek out from beneath. She took a deep breath and swiveled her head to see her lovers. Were they even now pulling off their pants to complete her rape?

In the moonlight, she saw several tiny figures, only slightly taller than the side of the bed. And from what she could make out in the shadowy moonlight, they had very large heads and tremendous eyes. They stood, still and silent, their necks craned, their faces pointed toward the ceiling. She wiggled her head against the pillow, and her blindfold came all the way off. She gasped as she realized that the men who had just done all that to her weren't human. Yet she wasn't frightened or disgusted.

"Can you explain?" she said softly.

Slowly, the creature who stood closest to her face turned and looked at her. "Oh, no," he said. "Your blindfold." It was Joe's voice.

"I can see that you're not human. Please tell me what's going on."

The creature who called himself Joe looked quickly at the others in the room, Maria couldn't tell how many. There was a soft chattering, then he turned back to her. "We may as well," he said sadly. "I am sorry you found out."

He reached over and turned on the lamp beside Maria's bed. In the brighter light, Maria could see that the creatures were a soft bluish color, with skin that looked slightly scaly. Except that they had almost human hands and faces. They weren't ugly, she realized, just really, really odd. "Please. Tell me. I think you owe me that."

"Yes. We do owe you much, and our gratitude as well." He sighed again. "Where we are from is too difficult to explain, so let us just say we are not from here. And we are trapped here. We landed several miles away a few of your weeks ago and have learned much from your television. It is an amazing creation."

Another of the aliens continued the story, his voice as rich and comforting as Joe's. "Our ship cannot take off again since we have too little power. But we discovered that sexual excitement, and particularly a woman's climax, creates a type of energy that we can absorb, then transfer to our ship. It is a bit difficult to explain any better than that."

A third picked up the story. As Maria looked around, she counted seven of the creatures surrounding her bed. "You are the second woman we have used like this. I am truly sorry, but we felt that we gave so much pleasure that it was not really stealing. And you do not use that energy anyway. You were not supposed to find out who we are."

"So your plan was just to disappear afterward?"

"Yes. And it worked the first time. But you got the blindfold off. That was a mistake. We must never let anything like that happen again, of course."

"And that's why you tied my hands, too."

"Of course. Had you reached out and touched one of us, you would have known immediately."

"But you're such wonderful lovers, why don't you just

tell someone. Any woman would be glad to have such talented sex partners."

"Yes, maybe. But the panic we would cause would overwhelm your planet, and we would be lost."

"Yeah. I guess you're right. It was so good. If you had asked, I would have gladly given you what you took."

The creature called Joe reached over and untied Maria's hands. "We are truly sorry. We never meant to hurt anyone."

"And you didn't. That was the best sex I've ever had." Suddenly Maria's mind was whirling, her entrepreneurial spirit rushing to the fore. "You know, we could both make out really well here." She pictured a sort of pleasure palace for women, a place where the only rules were you could not use your hands and you had to wear a blindfold. She knew women who would pay a fortune for sexual pleasure like she had just had. And these aliens would get all the energy they could use. It might work. It just might work. "I think I've got a plan."

# Blind Passion

## THE NEXT CHAPTER

WHAT THE HELL am I doing here, Dena Powell thought to herself. I must be out of my mind. She heaved a sigh and acknowledged that the waiting was driving her nuts. How had she gotten herself into this?

It had all started several weeks before, in the sauna at the racquet club. She had been soaking alone in the heat when Maria Marquez walked in, wrapped in a huge yellow towel. "Maria," she had said, standing to embrace her old friend. "I haven't seen you in months. How the heck are you?"

"Dena," the taller woman said, hugging her friend. "I'm fantastic. And you?"

"Not too bad." She dropped back onto the wooden bench, lying on her belly atop her striped towel. "I'm learning."

"I heard about you and Henry," Maria said, spreading her towel on the upper shelf and stretching out on her back. "How are you holding up?"

"Surviving. It's been almost four months."

"Dating?"

"Not now. It's taking me a while to adjust."

Maria winked. "Getting any?"

Dena barked a laugh. "Not a bit. I've almost forgotten

what good sex is like. I'm really not up to dating and all the rigmarole that goes with it."

"That doesn't preclude good sex, however."

"It doesn't? What's a nondating woman supposed to do, run up to some guy on the street and beg to get laid?" Dena sighed, then turned over and wiped the sweat from her body with the corner of the towel.

"Not exactly. What do men do under similar circumstances?"

"I'm not into meat markets and bar pickups. One-night stands are almost as complicated and as dangerous as dating. Not a chance."

"I wasn't referring to one-night stands. However, if men can go to prostitutes, then what about us women?"

"Dial a date? You've got to be kidding. Women don't do that sort of thing."

"And why not?"

"It's just not done. Male prostitutes? Please!"

"Not male prostitutes. Men who just want to please you. Men who know exactly what you want and how to make it good." She turned onto her stomach and looked down at her friend. "And they can."

"What do you know about it? Have you been indulging?"

"I have indeed. Actually, I've got a few guys working with me who really know what's what, and where's where. You mention what you like, and voilà. Orgasms to end all orgasms. No strings, no commitments. It's all purely therapeutic. Just to get the kinks out, so to speak."

Dena sat up and looked Maria in the eye. "You're serious."

"I sure am. I've started a business, and I've already got more than a dozen steady customers. I get a small sum each time, and the guys get what they want. Believe me, they just want to please. They are happy only if they can provide great, and I do mean *great*, sex. Actually, I guarantee the best sex you've ever had, and you pay afterward, only if you think what I've said is true." She raised an eyebrow. "Interested?"

"Not a chance."

Maria mentioned a quite reasonable dollar amount. "That's what I usually charge, but since we've known each other for so long, let me offer my friends' services to you for free. Visit one afternoon, and see what they can do for you."

"Thanks, Maria, but I don't think so."

"Sure. No problem. If you should change your mind, give me a call. I'm still at the old number, and I'll gladly make arrangements."

Dena thought about Maria's offer for a week, getting more and more excited and more and more confused by the hour. Her body wanted it. Badly. But her mind rebelled. It's so sleazy, so dirty. She remembered her sex with Henry, the best thing about their relationship. He had been a really good, creative lover, and together they had explored many different areas of sexuality. They had spent hours seeing how many orgasms each could experience. Nothing could ever be that good again. Could it? Maria had seemed so sure.

It was almost two weeks after the afternoon in the sauna when Dena called her friend. They had talked and gotten comfortable enough for Dena to share some of the areas of passion that she particularly enjoyed. "Come over to my place at five tomorrow, and I'll set it up. There are only two rules. You will have to be blindfolded. Several of my guys don't want to be recognized, so you'll have to fantasize about who they are. Maybe Sean Penn or Kevin Sorbo. You'll never know. That's part of the deal. Second, you may not touch them, but from what you've told me, that's no problem."

"You keep talking about men, plural. I'm not sure I want more than one person."

"You have to trust me. Our magic word is 'spaceship.' If you say it at any time, everything will stop and you can go home, no questions asked. You're completely safe. I know 'trust me' is a hackneyed phrase, but you just have to."

So here she was, lying naked, facedown on a workout bench in her friend's basement. She was, as Maria had warned her, blindfolded, and her arms and legs were tied to the legs of the bench. Her large breasts hung down on either side of the narrow leather padding. And she waited.

Suddenly something rustled and she felt earphones placed over her ears. Soft romantic music began, just loud enough to block out any other sounds from the room. She heard a wailing saxophone and a soft clarinet, sounding like a warm summer night. Now she could neither hear nor see. Something touched her upper lip and she smelled the scent of exotic spice. It filled her nostrils, making her head swim. She was in her own cocoon, surrounded by sensuality.

Suddenly something pinched her right nipple. Something was being clipped to it, tightly, almost painfully. There was no stroking, no kissing, no fondling. Just the clamp on her nipple. Another clip. Shards of pain, yet not pain rocketed through her, and she moaned. She felt the sparks echo through her pussy, opening her, causing moisture to flow from her core. She felt her lips swell and her clit harden. Muscles twitched, and her mound throbbed. She had told Maria about her love of the combination of pain and pleasure, a love that Henry had honed over their years together. Could anyone else bring out that part of her?

The clips on her nipples were pulled, dragging her nipples downward on either side of the bench. "Please," she said. Please what? Stop. Continue? She didn't know. She didn't care. And the melancholy saxophone wailed in her ears.

Alternate pulling and releasing had her body's responses sharpened to a fine edge. Soon she was trembling, wet and open, ready for the next step. But would he know what to do? He? They? She didn't care. The smell, the music, and the darkness combined to enhance one another. And the pain on her nipples pushed her ever higher.

She felt fingers opening her and something slowly penetrating her pussy. A dildo. Large. Filling. Pressing and opening. She wanted to resist. It was almost too big. It wouldn't. . . . Yet it did. Then it withdrew, and penetrated again.

Then a hand landed on one of her ass cheeks. The spank was more noise than substance, and the sound was muffled by the music from the earphones. More slaps. No rhythm. Long pauses, then two or three quick slaps. And the constant movement of the dildo. And the pulling on her nipples. Ever higher. Ever higher.

The men seemed to know exactly how to drive her higher, yet not let her near climax. How long? Minutes? Hours? Her cheeks became hot and supersensitive. Like the clips, the slaps were painful, yet not quite painful. It was pure pleasure. She had never liked serious pain, although she and Henry had gotten pretty deeply into this kind of play. Now it was just the right mix, the perfect spice.

Suddenly hands parted her cheeks and something slippery and cold was being spread on her anus. "No," she said. "Don't." Spaceship. That was the word she could use if she really wanted everything to end. Did she? "No," she said again.

Yes. It was happening. With the dildo now still in her pussy, filling her totally, something slender and cold was being pushed into her rear hole. Henry had tried anal sex once or twice, but she had never really been comfortable with it. Now, slowly being penetrated by a slim anal dildo, she felt opened as she had never been before. Her hips bucked, seemingly of their own volition. She thrashed her limbs to the extent allowed by her restraints. She arched her back, and her moans became deafening, even over the music in her ears.

"God," she shrieked, and the dildo sunk deeper into her rear passage. "Oh God." She could no more control her climax than she could control the objects invading her body. She came, unable to do anything but ride the tide of pleasure, ride it out long and hard, like a surfer riding a powerful wave farther and farther, hoping it would never reach the shore. Yet it did. Occasionally in her lovemaking, she could rise to more than one orgasm, but now she was so completely satiated that her body was capable of nothing more.

As she lay, totally spent, the objects were removed from her body and her wrists and ankles were unfastened from the legs of the bench. She lay, still blindfolded, for several minutes, then slowly roused herself and walked toward the shower she knew lay beyond the door. She would take a long hot shower and go home, knowing she would be back many more times.

In another area of the house, Maria sat, surrounded by four small creatures with scaly, bluish skin and overly large heads and eyes. The one who called himself Joe smiled. "That was the best yet," he said. "Her orgasm will fuel our ship for many miles of travel."

Maria marveled at their ability to harness such energy and transfer it to their marooned ship. "Do you need much more?" she asked, worried that they would soon be gone.

Their business was thriving, and no woman had ever failed to return.

He smiled softly, his strange features becoming almost handsome, for an alien. "We still need more energy, and we do so enjoy the way we get it. The thrill of feeling a climax like we do is as good as the actual orgasm."

Maria grinned back. "Well, we've got time before Nancy Stern gets here. How about coming up to my bedroom and I'll give you enough energy to travel to the moon? And back."

# The Corset

I WAS STANDING in front of a rack of Victorian corsets in my favorite sex shop, my cock flaccid, my mind wandering. I have several regular play partners, and I keep lots of luscious outfits for them, but I'm always on the lookout for new, exciting bits of erotic lingerie that I can share with my pets.

Yes, pets. Plural. I know it's not fashionable in this day and age to date more than one woman at a time, but I'm not ready to settle down to one flavor yet. Every one of my partners knows that she is not my one and only, and each is free to date anyone else she chooses. I always take care to use a condom, two if I want to play the back way, if you catch my drift, and I am sure to have myself tested for any nasty little germs at least four times a year. That's the way I choose to live, and, if others want to share my lifestyle, that's great. If not, that's fine, too.

Anyway, I was standing, fingering a particularly lovely satin corset, when a slightly shy-looking young woman walked into the shop. She looked around, obviously nervous about her first visit to a sex shop, then almost tiptoed toward the rack behind which I was standing. As she walked, I watched. She was a moderately pretty young woman, in her early twenties, I'd guess, with soft brown hair curling to her shoulders, large blue eyes, and a small, tight body. In her jeans and tank top, she looked like she was in good shape, but not overly muscled.

She saw me, looked at me for a moment, then turned away, blushing. Now I'm not at all bad to look at—tall, with black hair, deep brown eyes, and a body my pets call hunky. I smile at one woman's term for me. She refers to me as a major babe. As someone who prides himself on being very male, being a babe isn't my idea of a compliment, but she means it as such so I assume that women like what they see.

I think the young woman beside me did, too. "Good afternoon," I said softly. "I'm Clint."

When she remained silent, I said, "It's really okay to talk to strangers. My mother always said you never meet anyone truly exciting unless you occasionally take a chance."

I heard her soft chuckle. "I'm Gwen."

"Your first time here?" I asked.

"I used to come here a lot, but it's been a long time. I'm just looking."

Never one for much subtlety, I asked, "Did your boyfriend send you out to buy something special?"

"Oh no. We broke up two months ago. It was really bad. I guess that I'm just trying to feel feminine again." She didn't realize that she was stroking the smooth fabric of a tightly boned, midnight blue silk corset.

"I'm sorry that you two broke up, but it's probably for the best. I don't think he understood you."

"Excuse me?" Without realizing it, she continued to run her fingers over the stays, rigid and constricting.

"I think you want to feel something like that corset you're caressing on your body, the laces being drawn tighter and tighter."

She dropped her hand as if the corset had suddenly grown tentacles. "I beg your pardon?"

"That's a restraining garment. It gives the wearer the feeling of being tightly bound." I lifted the hanger from the rack and showed Gwen several small loops of fabric. "There are also places for bindings to be attached."

Gwen stared as I slowly inserted one finger into a loop, then withdrew it. Slowly, in and out, my finger fucked the loop. Her eyes never left my hand. I took an educated guess. "Your boyfriend didn't understand your needs, did he? Maybe he was pretty straight?"

"Very," she whispered.

"So why don't you try this on? There's a fitting room in the back."

"I'm sorry," she said, her voice trembling. "I think you have the wrong idea."

"I'm seldom wrong. I understand your hesitation, but it's really silly to deny something so obvious, and something that could give us both so much pleasure. I'd love to see you in that. Close your eyes and think about yourself in that corset, with me beside you. Give yourself the opportunity to have some fun and remember how good it used to be before your boyfriend loused it all up."

"But it's kinky."

Without overly pressuring her, I said, "And what's wrong with kinky, if it gives pleasure? Please."

She looked from the garment to my face, then back again.

"You'll be in a public place, and nothing can happen that you don't want. The clerk's an old friend of mine, and he will leave us alone. But if you call out, he'll be on me real quick. He won't jeopardize a customer, ever. I'm in here a lot, and I would endanger his friendly attitude if I got the least bit out of line." I paused, then whispered, "Please."

Without another word she nodded, took the corset from my hand, and walked toward the curtained-off rear of the store. I waited several minutes, then made eye contact with Brandon, the store's owner and clerk. He nodded, and I walked into the back.

In the corner of the storage area there was a large area separated from the rest of the room by heavy drapes. "Gwen?" I whispered.

"Yes," I heard from behind the drapes.

"May I see how that looks?" I wanted her full agreement.

"I can't get it fastened," she said. "I guess I could use some help."

I slipped through the drapes and just gazed at her. She had removed all her clothes and was almost wearing the blue corset. It had a line of hooks up the back, and she had closed only the bottom half. "Here," I said, "let me help you." I pulled the corset and fastened the remaining hooks, then looked into her eyes in the full-length mirror that covered two walls. "It's not nearly tight enough. Shall I show you?"

She stared at me, then nodded.

The laces were in the front so I moved between her and the mirror, then crouched and took the ends of the laces and wound them around my hands. I pulled. Hard, slowly, smoothly until I knew her waist was being tightly compressed. I moved so we could both see her. The sight was maximally erotic. The deep blue covered her from hips to breasts, with long blue garters dangling below. I could just make out her soft brown pubic hair. "More?" I whispered.

"Yes," she said. I pulled the laces tighter, and she gasped.

"Let me make this better," I said. I knew this garment well since I had several versions for my friends to wear, so I reached beneath Gwen's breasts and deftly removed the fabric that covered them.

"Oh," she said as two pieces of fabric came away in my hands. Now the corset pulled her ribs and waist tightly but fully revealed her small tight breasts.

"God, you're gorgeous in that." I whispered in her ear. "I want to show you more."

I could tell from her face that she was lost in an erotic fog. She couldn't speak, so I slipped out of the dressing room and returned quickly with other items from the store. I pulled a special pair of long black gloves onto her arms and clipped small hooks to the loops on the sides of the corset, effectively imprisoning her elbows against her sides. Her nipples were hard little buttons reaching forward. "Look at yourself," I said. "You're so beautiful, and so hot." I walked behind her and cupped her breasts. Then I pinched her nipples hard. "And you love it. Tell me how you love this."

"Oh God," she moaned.

"This is the real you. You've been trying to deny it, but it just won't work. You need it."

"Yes," she groaned. "I need this so much."

I reached down and unzipped the front of my jeans, allowing my now-rigid cock to spring free. "Show me how much."

Without hesitation, Gwen knelt and took my hard member into her soft mouth. "Slowly," I told her. "There's no hurry."

She sat back on her haunches and said, "Yes, there is. I want you."

I laughed. "Then you shall have me." There was a small straight chair in the corner of the room. I unfastened her elbows from the sides of the corset and fastened them together. Then I bent her forward and placed her hands on the seat of the chair. Her ass cheeks were beautiful with wisps of pussy hair visible. I quickly sheathed my cock in latex, then parted her cheeks. Unerringly, my erection found her pussy hole and I plunged inside. At the same time I reached around and roughly squeezed one breast with one hand. I found her clit with the other.

It took only a moment until she screamed and I felt the spasms of her pussy on my cock. That was all my heated flesh needed, and I came with a roar. After a few moments, I released her elbows and handed her my handkerchief so she could clean up her juices. I removed the condom and rezipped my pants. "I think you've learned about yourself today."

"Oh yes," she said, grinning. "It's foolish of me to pretend. I can't settle for less than what I need."

"I would like to get to know you better," I said. It had been so quick that I wanted time to savor her. "Just for fun and games, and anything else we can find."

"I think I'd like that. Maybe this time we could talk a bit before—"

I laughed. "You know, I think this is the beginning of something rather special."

"I hope so," she said. "How about we get some coffee?" She hesitated, looking down at the corset. "And get me out of this thing. . . . For the moment."

# The Gloves

IT MUST HAVE BEEN the gloves. I remember that night clearly, and it was the gloves. And the Bloody Marys.

Larry and I had been invited to a formal thing at his boss's country club, and I decided to wear a black strapless number that I had worn a few times before. To give it new life, I found a long, cream-colored silk scarf in a department store. I draped it around my neck and allowed the ends to trail down my back. I also found a pair of long, cream-colored satin gloves that came up well past my elbows to wear with the outfit. If I do say so myself, I looked smashing.

At the party, I felt different, somehow, sensuous and powerful. During the evening, we had a sumptuous meal, and I drank quite a few of those wonderfully spicy tomato juice concoctions. After dinner I danced with Larry's boss, and with several of his coworkers. All of them commented on how sexy I looked. I also danced with Larry several times, and he held me close and nibbled on my ear. It was fantastic.

We had hired a limo for the evening, knowing that we would probably drink a bit too much, so when we were ready to leave, there it was, waiting in front of the club, a uniformed chauffeur in the driver's seat. Giggling and knowing that we had the use of the limo for another hour, I said, "Let's drive around for a while." Then I leaned over and whispered to Larry, "Let's give the driver a bit of a show."

Now let me tell you that Larry is always willing for me to show off my body to men. He loves it when I wear a skimpy bikini and, on occasion, when I'm wearing a tight skirt, he's been known to have me remove my panties and spread my legs for anyone who might be watching. Tonight, he seemed willing to play.

"Hey, driver," he said, "drive north on the highway until you get to the state line, then turn around and drive back again." In a stage whisper he said, "That should take about an hour." Then he started kissing me—deep, tongue-dueling kisses that weakened my knees and moistened my pussy. "Are you getting hot?" he asked.

"Yes," I said, moving my hips to try to relieve the ache in my cunt.

"Then let's show the driver what he's missing." Deftly, Larry grabbed the zipper tab at the back of my dress and pulled it all the way down, allowing the top to fall to my waist. I was wearing my black strapless bustier that cinched my waist and lifted my ample tits. I watched as the driver moved his rearview mirror so he had a good view of the carryings-on in his backseat.

"He's watching," I said, rubbing my still-gloved hands over the silky fabric of the cincher.

"Oh yes," Larry said. "He's getting a good view. Show him those gorgeous tits."

I still had my gloves on, and my satin-covered hands against my skin made it feel as if someone else was touching my body, but touching it exactly where and how I wanted to be touched. I lifted my right breast out of the cup and held it for Larry to lick. "Yes, baby," I said as his head dipped toward my aching nipple. "Suck and lick it." I cupped the back of Larry's head with my gloved hand and massaged his neck as he suckled. With his face against my chest, I was able to make eye contact with the driver as he glanced in the mirror.

I rubbed my satiny fingers over Larry's cheeks as he nursed on my flesh. I unbuttoned his shirt and pulled it open, rubbing my hands over his smooth, hairless chest. My hands were everywhere. It was as if they had a mind of their own. I unzipped Larry's pants and pulled out his hard cock, stroking it, feeling it harden and swell.

"Ma'am," the driver suddenly said softly, his voice trembling a bit. "If you're going to keep doing things like that, I'd better pull over. I can't drive and watch, and I can't stop watching. I don't want us to end up in the hospital."

I put my hand beneath Larry's chin and lifted his face. "Let's have him pull over and watch," I said. "Is that okay with you?" I trusted that Larry wouldn't agree if something made him uncomfortable. He grinned, then whispered, "I am even willing to share if you want to."

Did I want to? I had always had fantasies about two men pleasuring me at the same time, but I never dreamed it might come true. But here I was, half-naked, wearing those incredibly sexy long gloves, Larry's cock in my hand, and a nice-looking man about to join us. "Pull over," I said, "in some private spot."

"I know this area. There's an old golf course just off this exit. I can park there where no one will see."

He quickly exited the highway, and soon we were parked in a darkened lot. "Now," I said, "if you really want to watch, why don't you come back here and see everything up close—" I giggled "—and personal, as they say on TV."

Quickly the driver flicked off the lights, tuned the radio to a soft music station, and moved into the backseat. "It's very dark," Larry said as the driver settled himself on the side opposite to where Larry was sitting. Two hot, hungry men, one on each side of me. I was in heaven.

The driver turned on one of those goose-neck reading lights found in some limos and moved the light so the bright, warm beam illuminated my swollen breast. I quickly freed the other one from my bustier. "What's your name?" I asked the driver.

"Chet," he said, his eyes glued to my hardened nipple.

"Want to play, Chet?" I asked, stroking his cheek with my gloved hand.

Silently, he raised his eyes and looked into mine. I cupped my right breast and offered it to my husband, who immediately started to nip at the tight nub. I cupped my left breast and looked at Chet. As if offered a feast, he bowed his head and took the nipple into his hot mouth. I leaned back on the leather seat, stroking the necks of two men as their mouths played havoc with my senses. Two mouths. Two sets of teeth. Two tongues. It was my fantasy, only better than I could have imagined. I closed my eyes and felt heat flow from my tits to my wide-open pussy.

The dress was split up the side so, as I allowed my legs to part, my thighs were exposed. Larry lifted his head. "She's got gorgeous legs," he said to Chet. "And they're so soft. Feel."

Larry slid his fingertips up the inside of my right thigh above my stockings, and, with little coaxing, Chet's hand began to stroke my left. I felt Chet's confidence in the whole situation grow, and his hand become bolder as he brushed the crotch of my soaked panties. As Chet's fingers began to work magic between my legs, Larry pinched my nipples.

"Oh God," I hissed.

"Yes, baby," Larry purred. "I'm pinching your tits while a

strange man is stroking your pussy. It makes you so hot, doesn't it?"

"Yes," I moaned, unable to think clearly anymore. My body was on fire, my pussy lips swollen and open, my cunt aching to be filled.

"Help me," Larry said to Chet. Together they lifted my ass and pulled off my panties. I stretched my legs out in the long body of the limo, my ankles wide apart. "Do you want to do her?" Larry asked Chet. "Not with your cock. I'll always keep that for myself, but with your hands and your mouth?"

Chet slid off the seat and crouched between my spread legs. "God, you've got a hot box, lady," he groaned, his mouth finding my clit, his fingers entering my pussy.

"Yes, yes, yes," I said. It was almost more than I could take. Larry kept pinching my nipples, just this side of severe pain, while Chet's mouth sucked and his tongue flicked and his fingers filled me. I came. I wanted to hold back, make it last, but I couldn't. I came hard and fast and long. Wave after wave of liquid heat washed over me, and I screamed.

The two men kept up the sensations until I literally had to tell them to stop. There was a bottle of champagne in a cooler tucked into a compartment under the seat, and Chet opened it. In silence, we drank some straight from the bottle.

After I had had a few minutes to calm down, I looked at Larry and took his hard cock in my still-gloved hand. He smiled as I turned and, with my other hand, unzipped Chet's fly and pulled out his immense cock. As I held each cock, I felt their weight. My husband's was shorter, but thicker, while Chet's was long and slender, with a dark purple head.

I slid my slippery hands all over the two cocks. "That's

dynamite," Larry said, panting. "Those gloves make it feel totally different."

"I just know you feel so good, ma'am," Chet said. "But I'm afraid if you keep doing that I'm going to mess up your clothes."

"She has others," Larry said. I turned and saw that his eyes were riveted on Chet's cock in my hand. "Do it," he moaned. "Make him come."

I caressed and rubbed, then slid my hand into his pants and cupped his balls. "Lady," he groaned.

Larry pulled at one of my gloves until it came off, wrapped it around his cock and rubbed the length of his erect shaft. "Do him," he said.

I used my ungloved hand to tickle Chet's balls while my gloved one continued its relentless manipulation of his cock.

"I'm gonna come if you keep that up," he moaned.

"I hope so," I said. "Come for me, baby. Let me watch you spurt all over. Show me. Let me watch you both come." This was heaven. Two men, stretched out in the back of the limo, cocks hard and hungry, Larry rubbing his with my glove, Chet moaning as I jerked him off. Breathing was heavy, bodies trembled, and, almost simultaneously, the two cocks erupted, spurts of thick white jism arching onto the floor of the limo.

A while later, we rezipped and rearranged. Wordlessly, Chet got out and returned to the driver's seat. We drove home in silence, Larry's arms around me. When we arrived at our house, Larry signed the charge slip and added a healthy tip for our partner in sex. "I have your number," Larry said. "I think you can be sure we'll be calling on your—" he paused "—services again."

"I certainly hope so," Chet said as he slowly pulled away.

# *Family Jewels*

## ONE EVENING

**B**RAD AND I have been married for almost three years, and I'm still amazed by how sexy he is. Like Superman, beneath his mild-mannered exterior beats the heart of a hot, hungry sex maniac, and I'm beginning to think he's turned me into a fiend as well. We make love almost every night, and we have both become very creative at teasing and game playing.

One Saturday afternoon about a month ago, I was cleaning out an old closet, and I found the hand-decorated shoe box I used to keep all my junk jewelry in during high school. It had been five years since I had last rummaged in my treasures, so I sat on the hall floor and removed the lid from the box. With a wistful smile, I grabbed a handful of beaded necklaces.

I leaned against the wall and recalled the afternoons I spent with friends wandering through the local discount store, stocking up on plastic jewelry. During my senior year in high school, I even got a job in the cosmetics department, not only for the salary but also for the ten percent discount I got.

Sighing with pleasure at the memory, I filled my fingers with earrings, bracelets, and necklaces in a rainbow of colors, gold and silver. Many of the pieces were encrusted with rhinestones and chips of colored glass, and several of the gaudy rings had huge stones and fake pearls. Buried at the bottom were a few neck chains on which I used to hang charm holders and pendants engraved with my name or initials and tiny replicas of animals, shoes, or hearts.

As I picked up a pair of long, dangly golden earrings, I started thinking. I smiled and began rushing around the house. I knew I had to hurry if I was going to be ready by the time Brad got home from doing his errands.

In the back of one of my bureau drawers I found several large silky scarves. After stripping off all my clothes, I wrapped one around my ample breasts and put aside another to cover the lower half of my face. I snapped two golden chains together and fastened them around my waist, then draped one large scarf over the waist chain in the front and another in the back. I put on a pair of dangly golden earrings, pinned an ornate necklace into the top of my long brown hair so it hung over my forehead, and covered my arms with harem-style bracelets. I hung three heavy beaded necklaces around my neck, fastened several bracelets around my ankles, and put a ring on each finger. To complete the outfit, I added bright red lipstick and heavy, dark green eyeshadow. As I heard Brad slam the front door I bobby-pinned the scarf in place over the lower half of my face.

"Sandy!" Brad yelled, "I'm home."

"In here," I answered. "In the bedroom." I struck a seductive pose and waited. Brad walked into the room, and I watched his eyes roam over my body. I could see what he saw reflected in the mirror behind him. My nipples were hard and showed clearly through the scarf that tried unsuccessfully to hold them. My dark, fluffy pubic hair made a slight bulge in the front of the scarf that hung between my knees. As I looked at my husband and slowly moved my hips, I saw a matching bulge appear in the front of Brad's jeans.

"Sit down and don't move a muscle," I said, my breath making the face scarf flutter against my lips. "You're in for a show." I pushed Brad down onto the foot of the bed, turned on the radio, and turned it to an easy-listening station.

I picked up the beat of a soft-rock song and began to dance around the room, watching Brad's eyes follow my every move. I pinched my nipples through the silky fabric and then slid my palms over their pebbled tips.

"Oh, Sandy," Brad said. "You make me so hot." I watched him shift position to make more room for his cock inside his tight jeans.

"Poor darling," I breathed. I danced over to him and unzipped his pants. He tried to reach out for me, but I whispered, "I told you not to move." I fumbled with his underwear and pulled out his hard, throbbing cock. "I just want to give him some air," I said, slipping the tip under my face scarf and planting a lipsticked kiss on the end. Then I blew a stream of cool air over his exposed erection. "That should help."

Slowly, I reached behind my back and untied the scarf that covered my breasts. Holding the multicolored fabric against my nipples, I rubbed back and forth against it, arching my back like a cat in heat.

I slowly slid the wisp of fabric across his face, then kissed his mouth through the two layers of silk. "Filter-tip kissing," I whispered. "That's all for now." I dropped the scarf that had tied my tits onto the bed.

Now that my breasts were freed from their confinement, I wriggled my shoulders so that they swayed and bounced before Brad's hungry eyes. As my hips undulated, I reached around and grasped the end of the scarf that hung from my waist in back. I brushed the silken fabric over the end of

Brad's huge cock, then again kissed the tip of his organ through the material. "Not unfiltered just yet," I said, my breath heavy and hot against the silk. I slid my hand up and down his covered shaft until I could see a small drop of pre-come form. Then I handed the end of the scarf to him. "Just hold that, baby," I told him, then slowly backed away until the scarf slid from the waist chain.

Knowing that my firm ass was now bare, I turned and shimmied, then grabbed my cheeks and pulled them apart, giving my husband a good view of my puckered hole.

"Oh, honey," Brad moaned, "you're killing me." I knew that he was thinking about ass fucking, one of his favorite pleasures. He was suffering the delicious torment of being teased and loving every moment of it.

With my back still facing Brad, I took the end of the scarf that covered my pussy in the front, and handed it to him between my legs. "Now you get to play," I said to him. He knew exactly what I wanted. What we both wanted.

"I love playing with you," Brad said, sliding the end of the scarf up the insides of my thighs. "So stand still, baby, and let me play." He raised his hand, lifting his end of the scarf, pressing the material against my wet pussy. Then, as he slowly pulled the scarf from the waist chain, it slid between my swollen lips and rubbed against my hard clit.

"Getting hot, too, darling?" Brad asked.

"Oh yes," I whispered as I turned around. "But today it's my party. Lie back."

As he lay back on the bed I admired the exaggerated contrast between us. He lay there, still fully dressed, with his cock standing at full attention and sticking through the fly of his jeans. I was naked, with a scarf over my face and dozens of pieces of jewelry adorning my body. I loved it just this way. As Brad started to unbutton his shirt, the scarves gave me an idea.

"Don't," I said. His hands froze, and he watched me pick up one of the lengths of silk. "Now, give me your wrist." Brad held out his right arm, his eyes gleaming. I looped the end of one scarf around his wrist, quickly tying it to one side of the bed frame. We'd tried light bondage for the first time about a month earlier, and it had led to a wild night of uninhibited fucking. To make sure everything was okay now, I looked into Brad's eyes. I smiled at the unrestrained lust I saw, then walked to the other side of the bed and quickly tied his other wrist.

"Now, baby," I purred, "let's see how much you want me." I leaned over and tickled the end of his exposed cock with one long earring. I watched as another drop of fluid oozed out. "Oh yes, that's good. I want you to want me very much." I climbed onto the bed and, with one knee on either side of his chest, dangled one breast above his open mouth.

"Want to suck me?" I asked.

"Oh baby," he whispered, his breathing so heavy that he was barely able to get the words out.

I let my engorged nipple brush his lips, then I filled his mouth with my flesh. "Suck it good, honey," I said. "Suck it good." His mouth tugged rhythmically at my sensitive nipple and made my pussy quiver and twitch. I had to have him, yet I wanted to continue to tease. Without pulling my tit from his mouth, I lowered my body until my wet labia touched the end of his cock. I reached between my legs, wrapped my hand around his throbbing erection, and rubbed it against my clit.

"Baby," Brad said, my tit slipping from his mouth, "let me fuck you."

"You suck, I'll do the fucking." I put my other nipple in his mouth, and he resumed almost nursing at my breast. I continued rubbing his cock against my clit until I thought I would explode from the pleasure of it, then I placed Brad's purple cock head at the opening of my sopping cunt, and inch by slow inch, I allowed my body to drop. Gradually his pole filled me. I could feel his muscles tense as he pulled at the scarves holding his arms. He wanted to control our fucking, but he quickly realized that since he couldn't use his arms, I was in charge.

Suddenly his hips bucked, trying to take me more quickly than I wanted. I pulled back and glared at him. "Bad boy," I said. "This is my party."

His eyes glowed hungrily, but he smiled at me. "I want your hot and wet pussy surrounding my cock. Please," he said.

"I like that," I said. "Ask nice."

"Please, baby. Let me fill you up."

I leaned back and slowly lowered my pussy onto his shaft. Then I held completely still and felt his cock twitch and wiggle deep inside of me. "Like that?" I asked sweetly, knowing he wanted much more.

He hesitated. I knew he wanted me to move and fuck his cock, but he said, "Whatever you want, baby."

"Well right now, I want you bad." I raised my body, then dropped onto his cock. Quickly, I established a rhythm, raising my hips, then impaling myself on his prick. Over and over I fucked him, until I knew I was almost there. I reached down and fingered my clit, then exploded as his cock spurted deep inside my hot pussy. My hips bucked against Brad's as we both screamed our climax.

I quickly untied Brad's wrists, and we lay together. "You know, baby," Brad said, "that was terrific. But I'll get back at you for teasing me."

I knew he would, and I looked forward to it. But I never dreamed that my jewelry would give him the means.

# *Family Jewels*

## A FEW DAYS LATER

A FEW DAYS LATER, I arrived home from work to find that Brad had picked up our favorite Indian food from a local restaurant. To go with the spicy-hot food, we consumed several bottles of cold beer. After dinner, Brad said, "I liked the way you looked naked, in all that jewelry the other night. Would you dress up for me like that again tonight?"

After we cleaned up the dinner remains, we went into the bedroom. "I want you naked," he said, and I willingly obliged. Then he took out the shoe box and handed me necklaces, earrings, and bracelets for both my wrists and ankles. He even gave me a waist chain, which I put around my middle. "Like this?" I asked.

"You look wonderful. Now lie down."

From the gleam in his eye, I knew he had something devilish in mind, and I was eager to know what it was. Sensuously, I stretched out on the bed, naked except for my adornments.

Brad picked up a small safety pin from the bed table. "Now, to continue." He took the pin and, carefully so I didn't get stuck, slid it through one of my bracelets and used it to pin my wrist to the sheet so my arm was straight out at shoulder level. Quickly, he similarly pinned my other wrist.

"Those bracelets are very flimsy," Brad purred, "and you could pull free at any time if—" he hesitated "—you wanted to break them. But they're very valuable, and you wouldn't want them broken, would you?"

"Oh no," I whispered, playing the game that my dime-store jewelry was somehow worth millions. It was strange and highly exciting, lying here, naked, covered with jewelry, while Brad was still fully dressed.

"I think you need more jewelry," he said, taking a strand of orange beads from the box. He opened the clasp and wrapped the necklace around my upper thigh so the cool beads just brushed my pussy hair. Then he slipped the necklace through the waist chain and fastened the clasp. "Now, you wouldn't want to break any of these, so don't move suddenly," he said, a leering smile on his face. He quickly wrapped a purple strand around my other thigh and slid it through the waist chain as well. It was a strange feeling, like being chained up. And it was almost as though the beads were pulling my pussy lips apart. I was breathless, my body quivering from the hunger that was flowing through my veins.

"Good," Brad purred. "Very good." He surveyed my body. "Now for your ankles." He looped a string of hot pink beads through an ankle bracelet on one leg and a navy blue one through a chain on the other. Then he drew both necklaces up through the waist chain, forcing my legs to bend at the knees. The only way to get my legs comfortable was to let them fall open so that my soaked pussy was exposed, framed in colored beads.

"Oh, I like the way that looks," Brad said. "I bought a few necklaces of my own today," he said, "and I cut open the strings." He chuckled. "Of course, I didn't want to destroy the valuable ones." I smiled at his joke. Then Brad showed me a bowl filled with loose, colored plastic beads, and he ran his fingers through his hoard.

He dug into the bowl, took a handful of beads, and held them over my breasts. Slowly, he let them pour through his spread fingers and fall soft and cool on my heated flesh. Gently, he again filled his hands with beads and used them to caress and massage my globes, ribs, and belly. He covered my body with the round pieces of plastic and rolled them everywhere.

"I want you to know that I've washed all of these thoroughly." I didn't have long to wonder why he'd said that. He held a string of pearly white beads, slid them down my belly, and dangled them against my pussy hair. "There's one place you don't have jewels yet," he said, then knelt between my spread knees. One bead at a time, he inserted the entire strand of pearls into my soaking cunt. The feeling was so erotic that it was hard not to come right then.

"Now, I can't leave them in there too long," he said, "or they might be damaged." He leaned over, his mouth close to my swollen lips. "Let me see if I can find them."

He looked for the beads, all right, with his tongue. He slowly explored every fold of my cunt, murmuring occasionally, "Not here." He slid his lips over my hard clit. "Not here either." Then his tongue found the small loop of beads that he had left protruding from my pussy. "There they are," he purred, his breath hot on my wet skin.

I felt him catch the loop with his tongue and grasp it with his teeth. Bead by bead he pulled the pearls out of my pussy. "I'm going to come," I screamed.

"Not just yet, baby." Leaving the pearls still partly inside of me, Brad quickly pulled off his clothes. I could tell by his straining cock that this torture was as exciting for him as it was for me. "I want to try one more thing before I fuck you," he said. He picked up all the loose beads and refilled the bowl. Then he knelt over the bowl and plunged his cock into the beads. "I knew it would feel sensational," he said, withdrawing and inserting his cock over and over again. I watched him fuck the bowl of plastic beads, one or two beads sticking to the wet, sticky end of his big, hard rod. "They feel so cool as they slide over my hot prick."

It was almost torture watching him as he fucked the bowl of beads for a full minute. I wanted his cock inside of me, and I could tell he was getting very close. "Save that for me," I said.

"Don't worry, baby," Brad said, showing me his eager cock. "This is all for you."

He crouched between my spread knees and rubbed the exposed loop of pearls over my cunt, paying special attention to my hardened clit. I was so hot I yelled, "Fuck me now."

"Bad girl," he said, smiling. "This is my party now." He leaned down and took the bead loop with his teeth and again began to pull the rest of the strand from my pussy. When the last bead finally popped from my body, he leaned over and teased me with his prick. Then, inch by inch he inserted his cock into me.

I was beyond caring about my "valuable jewelry." I pulled on the necklaces holding my ankles and quickly broke them both. I wrapped my legs around Brad's waist and drove him hard into my body, enjoying the odd pressure of the beads that surrounded my upper thighs. As I pulled him hard inside of me a second time, I came. Brad came only moments later.

Later, lying next to each other, our breathing slowly returned to normal. "Well, baby," Brad said, holding up the two broken necklaces, "you've broken two pieces of the family jewels."

I grabbed his now flaccid cock. "The family jewels are just fine. But we'll have to go to the store and buy some more plastic beads. I want a rematch."

"So do I, baby. So do I."

# In the Shower

HE'S GOING to be home in just a few hours, Jenny thought as she opened the apartment door and dumped the groceries on the kitchen table. Steak, baked potatoes, salad, and asparagus. She arranged the ingredients for a good, home-cooked meal on the counter. And, she thought, grinning, me for dessert.

Jenny's husband, Karl, had been away for almost three weeks on a business trip and, having wrapped up a big sale, was due home on a flight landing at five-thirty. She checked to see whether the flight was landing on time and was glad that everything was on schedule. "Let's see," Jenny mumbled, "landing at five-thirty, an hour to get his luggage and clear customs, and half an hour from the airport to here. Seven. So I'll plan dinner for seven-thirty, but I won't put the steak on until he's home."

She looked again at her watch. Five-forty. He should be pulling up to the gate. I've got time for a quick shower, and then I'll get organized. Leaving all the groceries on the counter, Jenny walked into the bedroom and stripped off her work clothes. Dressed in only her bra and panties, she walked into the bathroom and adjusted the shower until the temperature was just right. She quickly pulled off her underwear and stepped beneath the pounding water. With a long sigh, she let the water beat on the back of her neck. With her back to the shower curtain, she began to soap her body.

Suddenly she heard a sound behind her and felt cool air on her wet back. "Guess who?"

"Karl, baby," she said, placing her hand over her pounding heart. "You startled the hell out of me." She turned and saw that her husband of four years was naked and had stepped into the shower. "I didn't expect you until about seven," she said, calming her breathing.

"I couldn't wait to get home, so I managed to catch an earlier flight. I wanted to call, but I just had no time. I dashed and just made it as the doors were closing. Sorry I'm early?"

"Oh, baby, not at all." She wrapped her arms around her husband and held him against her wet, naked body. Her mouth found his, and they kissed as the water pounded around them. As they parted, she said, "I missed you so much."

Karl grabbed her hand and put it on his swollen cock. "I missed you, too." He took the bar of soap and rubbed it in his hands. When he was all lathery, he said, "You wanted to wash before I got home, and I wouldn't want to stop you." He held her against him and used his soapy hands to rub her back. He kneaded her muscles and rubbed up and down the length of her spine. Adding more lather, he cupped her ass cheeks and pulled them apart as he also pressed her mound against his hard cock.

"Umm," she purred, "that feels so good."

"It sure does. Now turn around." As Jenny turned, Karl again lathered his hands. She pressed her back against his chest and wiggled her soapy butt against his crotch. His palms found her breasts, and his slippery hands lifted her heavy tits and rubbed the nipples. He rolled first one hardening bud then the other between his fingers.

Jenny felt her knees almost give way beneath the sensual onslaught. His hands were everywhere, slick and slippery, massaging and inflaming. Again and again he relathered his hands and found new places to rub. He knelt on the shower floor and rubbed her legs and feet, then ran his hands up the insides of her thighs.

"I've got to get you all clean," Karl said, rinsing his fingers, then sliding them between her legs, rubbing the places now slippery with her juices. "All over."

Playfully, Jenny pushed his hands away and then soaped hers. "You know," she said, her breathing ragged, "you've been flying for several hours, probably got all dirty and sweaty." She pulled him back to a standing position and rubbed his hairy chest. "Two can play this game."

She rubbed and caressed Karl's body with slippery hands, adding more soap from time to time. She stroked his back, his buttocks, his legs, his arms, and his neck, avoiding his cock and balls. With an impish grin, she said, "I'm sure you need to get clean all over."

Hot water cascading over her head, she lathered her hands and knelt on the bathtub floor. Carefully insinuating her fingers in every crevice, she soaped his balls, then his fully erect cock. As she washed him, she thought about oral sex. She knew that Karl wanted her to suck him, but every time she had thought about it in the past, it had made her gag. Now, however, with his cock at eye level, all soapy and clean, she thought she might be able to do it, or at least lick him, and what better welcome home gift for him.

She turned him so the water flowed over his belly and cock, then, when he was all rinsed, turned him again until his back was to the water. Then she said, "You know, eventually I have to dry you off. Why not start now?" She licked the length of his cock, tasting the clean water that covered him. As she licked, she cupped his testicles in her hand. "Umm," she purred. "You really taste good."

Jenny felt Karl's body tense as she again ran her tongue the length of the underside of his erection. "Oh God," he moaned. "You don't have to do that, you know."

"I know."

"Baby, it feels so good."

"I know that, too." A small bit of fluid flowed from the tip of her husband's prick, so Jenny tentatively touched her tongue to it. Tangy and salty, she thought, but not unpleasant. She pressed the flat of her tongue against the tip of his cock and licked. Not unpleasant at all. Could she go further? she wondered. Could she actually suck it into her mouth? Well, she thought, nothing ventured.

She formed her lips into an O and pressed her mouth to the head of Karl's throbbing member. The head popped into her mouth, then she drew back and it pulled out again. She did this several times, until she felt Karl lean back. "Baby," he said, "that's the most wonderful thing you could do, but you better stop before you get a mouthful of me."

I don't think I'm ready for that, she thought, but this isn't nearly as bad as I had expected. Karl grabbed her by her armpits and pulled her up, then knelt down and put his mouth against her pubic mound, finding her clit with his tongue. The sensations were electric, and Jenny was quickly aroused to the point of near-orgasm. Obviously knowing her arousal level, Karl stood and pressed her back against the wall of the shower. As the water poured over them, he lifted one of her legs, supporting her weight with his large body. Then he drove his cock into her waiting pussy.

He thrust again and again, driving her higher, pressing her back against the wall. "Yes, baby," he moaned. "Oh yes."

She dug her fingernails into his ass cheeks, pulling him still closer. With matching screams, the two climaxed almost simultaneously.

Panting and almost unable to stand, the two quickly rinsed off any lingering soap, climbed out of the shower, and, wrapped in fluffy towels, collapsed onto the bed. "Oh baby," Karl moaned. "That was sensational. I never expected you to do that."

"Me neither," Jenny said, her pulse slowly returning to normal, "but it just seemed right. Was what I did okay?"

Karl's chuckle was deep and warm. He pulled her close. "It was wonderful, baby. And any time you want to do it again, in or out of the shower, I'm willing. Eager. But if you don't, that's fine, too."

"Yeah," she said. "I know that. That's why I could do it, and it was really okay."

"You're fantastic." Just then his stomach rumbled. "You're also a great cook, you know."

Jenny giggled. "Okay. I get the hint."

"And after dinner," Karl said, "I want you for dessert."

"Exactly what I had in mind."

# The Mile-High Club

IT HAD BEEN a long period of frustration for my husband, Mark, and me. Together we owned and operated Littleton's Imports, and we had been traveling through the Far East on a buying trip for almost twelve days. We had had almost no privacy and had spent most of our time so tired that we had little desire for each other anyway. With no one in the third of the three-across seats, we'd managed to get comfortable enough on the flight home to doze long enough that we were both a bit more rested. We had four more hours until we landed, and we were really hungry for each other.

It had been chilly earlier so we were both covered by those soft bright blue blankets the airline had supplied, and we were still a bit blitzed from the drinks so frequently supplied by the accommodating flight attendants. The cabin was dark, the only illumination coming from a few reading lights. "Now that I've slept a bit," Mark whispered, "I find I'm horny as hell."

I sighed. "Me, too," I said softly. "I can't wait till we get home."

"Do we have to wait?"

"I'm not really quite up to joining the mile-high club," I said reluctantly. "Those tiny bathrooms just won't do, I'm afraid."

I felt Mark's hand slide up and down the thigh of my jeans. "I wasn't thinking of the bathroom."

"Don't be ridiculous," I said, horrified yet excited at the thought of doing it right here. And almost hungry enough to consider it. But not quite. "Not a chance, buster." His hand was probing the crotch of my jeans, rubbing and stroking through the heavy fabric. I could feel him, yet it was sort of muffled, really sexy. Playfully, I swatted his hand away. No way was I letting him paw me with a plane full of half-awake people and wandering flight attendants. "Come on, baby," I moaned. "Give a girl a break."

"You know you want it," he whispered hoarsely.

"Of course I do. But I'm not one for doing it in public, and this is about as public as it gets."

"But with this blanket over us, who'd know?"

I realized that he wasn't talking about actually fucking, just little play. Could I?

Mark reached over and tightened my seat belt until it was constricting my belly. He knew that things tight around my waist made me crazy. He leaned his mouth close to my ear. "What if you can't move?" he purred. "You're my prisoner, and you can't do anything about it."

God he can make me hot almost instantly. He knows me too well. I shuddered.

"Push up the armrest between us. Do it." His voice was a whisper, but the strength beneath it had me raising the armrest. "Good girl. Now put your hands on the seat beside you and don't move them."

Trembling I did as he instructed. Then I felt him unzipping my jeans and sliding his hand down my belly over my panties. "Wait," he said, pulling his hand back. "Where's your pocketbook?"

"Under the seat," I murmured, nodding to the seat in front of me.

He fumbled beneath the seat and pulled out my purse. He stared inside, then removed the small pair of scissors I always carry. "This will do nicely."

"What are you doing, you idiot?" I said.

"You'll see," he whispered, and stuffed my purse back beneath the seat. "Now put your hands back where I told you to keep them, and don't move." He reached beneath the blanket and found the opening in the front of my jeans. By feel, he placed the scissors into the leg opening of my panties and cut across the crotch. When he had completely severed the cloth, he cut up the front of the panties. He removed the scissors and dropped them in his shirt pocket. Then he pushed the crotch of the panties down between my thighs and said, "Lift up. The easier you make this, the less chance of anyone seeing."

Without thinking, I lifted my bottom off the seat, and Mark reached into the small of my back, grabbed the waistband of my panties, and pulled. With a bit of wiggling he managed to work my panties loose and pull them off completely. "That's better. I'll just hang on to these." He put the cut-up panties in his lap, beneath the blanket.

"But what will I do when it's time to get off?" I asked, half-indignant and half-delighted.

"Go naked underneath your jeans, I guess," Mark said, an idyllic expression on his face. "Now, where were we?" He slipped his hand into the open front of my jeans and found my pubic hair. "Ah yes." When I moved my hips, he hissed, "Don't move unless I tell you." He gazed into my eyes and knew just what buttons to push. "You're a slut and you know you like this. So sit still."

God, every time he calls me a slut, and he uses that magic word only in the heat of passion, it makes me crazy. "Yes, sir," I whispered.

A handsome male flight attendant walked down the aisle with a tray of plastic cups full of water. As he approached, Mark's finger wormed its way through my pubic hair.

"Would you like some ice water?" the flight attendant asked.

At that moment, Mark's finger found my clit. "Dear?" he said. "Water?" He rubbed, knowing I was now almost incoherent with lust.

"No, thanks," I said, choking out the words.

"And you, sir?" the attendant asked.

"Yes, please," Mark said, still rubbing. He reached out with his other hand and took a plastic cup. "Thanks."

As the flight attendant continued his rounds, Mark took a few swallows. Then he pulled his hand out of my crotch, swished his fingers in the cold water, and said, "Pull your jeans down over your hips and spread your legs as wide as you can. Do it, slut!"

His wonderful, commanding voice gave me no choice. I wiggled my jeans down, spread my legs, and closed my eyes, knowing what he was planning. Could I keep from screaming? He arranged the blanket so he had a clear path to my crotch, then took an ice cube from the water. With agonizing slowness, he moved the cube to my clit and touched me with it. Clamping my lips together so I wouldn't scream, I felt the first spasms of orgasm rock through me.

It was obvious what I was feeling so he quickly filled my pussy with his fingers, leaving the ice against my heated flesh. "Don't yell," he whispered, knowing how loud I usually am. When it appeared that I couldn't hold back, he pressed his mouth over mine, swallowing my shouts.

He kept rubbing and thrusting until I finally calmed a

bit. "My turn," he whispered. Then, slightly louder, he said, "Why don't you just stretch out across the three seats and take another nap?" I raised the other armrest and lay across the three seats with my head in Mark's lap. He artfully tented the blanket so my mouth and his lap were concealed. Then he unzipped his jeans and worked his erect cock out of the fly in his shorts. "Suck it, slut," he growled softly.

Eagerly I surrounded his prick with my hot lips, bouncing my head up and down on his shaft. As I sucked, I realized he was still holding the glass of ice water. I quickly grabbed it, took a cube in my mouth, and returned to his cock. As I knew it would be, the cold of the ice against his steaming prick was just too much, and he came, filling my mouth with his come. Luckily, I was able to swallow it all or he'd have had a large wet spot on his lap.

Minutes later, we sat up and straightened our clothing. "Does that mean we're members of the mile-high club?"

"I guess we are," Mark said with a grin. "And we'll be higher still when we get home."

"I can't wait."

# Atlantic City Gamboling

BILL AND KATHY had been spending overnights in Atlantic City for many years. They found that they particularly enjoyed the poker machines and could spend hours sitting next to each other betting quarters on the outcome of each new deal. They looked over each other's shoulders as they drew to royal flushes and four or five of a kind.

Late one evening, Bill's machine dealt him the ten, jack, king, and ace of spades, and the seven of clubs. "This isn't a bad hand," he said, tapping Kathy on the shoulder.

Kathy looked at his screen and grinned. "Not at all," she said, as Bill pushed the hold button beneath the four good cards.

"It would be nice, but it's next to impossible." Although he knew it well, he looked up at the payoff list. "One thousand coins. That's two hundred and fifty dollars."

"Don't count your money yet, love."

"I'm not." His finger poised over the deal button, he said, "I know it's a long shot, but how about a bargain. If this doesn't come in, you are mine to do with what I wish for an hour before we go to bed."

"Okay, and if it does you have to buy me the best dinner in town with all your winnings."

"Done," Bill said, pressing the button. The seven of clubs became the jack of diamonds. "Ah well, at least I have a paying pair."

They played the machines for another hour, had a few good hands, and finally cashed in and headed for the elevators having lost about ten dollars between them for the evening. "Nightcap?" Bill asked.

"Nah. I had three of those delicious Bloody Marys at the machine. I'm a bit tipsy as it is."

Bill pushed the elevator button and said, "You know you owe me an hour of servitude."

"Huh?" Kathy said.

"You mean you've forgotten our bet? The royal flush earlier?"

"Oh. Right. I didn't really think you were serious."

As the elevator doors opened, Bill leered at his wife. "I most certainly was serious." He remembered a story he had read once and decided to make it come true. "I changed my mind. I don't care whether you want a nightcap or not. You're mine now for the next hour, and I get to call the shots." Bill pushed the button that would take them to the restaurant floor.

Kathy grinned and shrugged. "You masterful fool, you," she said.

They arrived at the bar and made their way to a small table in the corner. Bill ordered two Bloody Marys. As the waiter left, Bill said, "Go into the ladies' room and remove your bra and panties and bring them to me."

"What?" Kathy gasped. Their sex play had frequently been delightfully creative, but this was a new twist.

"You heard me. Just do it."

"But—"

"Welshing on a bet?"

"No, but . . ." The idea was titillating but a bit scary.

Because it was midsummer, Kathy was wearing a light, knit tank top and a flowing print skirt. The casino was always well air-conditioned, so she had brought along a sweater.

Bill raised an eyebrow, and Kathy stood up and walked to the ladies' room. In a stall she removed her pink satin and lace bra, pulled her tank top back on over her large breasts and tightly erect nipples. She removed her light pink satin panties and put both garments into her purse. Then she walked from the stall and looked at her barely concealed body in the mirror. Quickly she pulled on her cardigan sweater and, blushing slightly, returned to the table.

As she approached, Bill could read the arousal on her face. He looked around. There were several couples talking quietly, and a waiter and barman in conversation at the other side of the room. Before Kathy could sit down in the chair opposite him, he said, "Take off that sweater."

"Bill—"

"Do as I say," he hissed, getting a charge out of her slight embarrassment. "You're always a bit prim, except in the bedroom, of course." To Bill, Kathy really did seem to be two different people. In public she was properly dressed and made up, but in the bedroom she was an experimenter and wonderfully aggressive partner. As he thought back, Bill realized that this was the first time he'd ever "been in charge."

"I won that bet fair and square. You promised."

"But there are other people here."

"We haven't been here in months and probably won't be here again for months more."

"But . . ."

To Bill's again raised eyebrow, Kathy slowly removed her sweater. Bill looked at his wife's body, his cock hardening in his pants at the sight of her large breasts revealed quite clearly through her light tank top. "When you sit down, I want you to pull up your skirt so your bare bottom is on the chair. You can do that subtly so no one else knows what you're doing."

Kathy sat down, arranging her skirt as she had been told. "That's cold," she said. She leaned over and added in a whisper, "And I'm so wet. This feels really weird."

"If you like you can put one of these napkins between you and the chair."

"No thanks."

The waiter arrived and put their drinks on the table. "Do you have anything to nibble on?" Bill asked. "You used to have those delicious bread sticks."

"We still do, sir," the waiter said. "I'll get you some."

As he left, Bill told his wife, "Give me your underwear."

Slowly, Kathy removed her bra and panties from her purse and surreptitiously handed them to Bill under the table. As she saw the waiter fill a wicker basket with bread sticks, she watched her husband spread the garments on the table. Horrified but fascinated by this new role her husband was playing, she watched the waiter walk toward the table. As the waiter held the basket out, Bill pointed to the crotch of Kathy's panties, spread on the white linen tablecloth. "Right here," he said, tapping the wisp of satin.

The waiter looked at the pink satin, then at Kathy. "Certainly, sir," he said, his expression unchanged. "Whatever you say." He put the basket on Kathy's panties.

Bill handed him a twenty-dollar bill. "We'd like two glasses of water, too."

Not knowing what else to do, Kathy sipped her drink as the waiter poured two glasses of water at the bar and returned to the table. Bill tapped his finger on her pink lacy bra and the waiter put one glass of water on each cup. "Thank you," Bill said.

"Yes, sir," the waiter said and, seeming reluctant, left. Kathy watched him quickly approach the barman and whisper to him. The two men looked in her direction and laughed.

"Now," Bill said, "skootch your chair around here next to me." There were only two chairs at the tiny table, so Kathy was easily able to move beside him, now facing the waiter and barman across the room. Bill pulled up her skirt and reached one finger into her now-sopping pussy. He found her hard clit and rubbed until Kathy's hips could hardly hold still.

"Stop that," Kathy said, barely able to catch her breath. "Stop."

"What did you say?" Bill asked, rubbing more quickly. "You have nothing to say here. Sit quietly until I tell you to do something."

With shaking hands, Kathy took another sip of her drink.

While Kathy, the waiter, and the barman watched, Bill opened a package of bread sticks and withdrew a long, slender rod. "Tip your pelvis up. Do it!" As she moved, Bill broke the rod in half with obvious flourish, then reached under the table. Before Kathy could protest, he inserted the stick into her cunt. Then he resumed rubbing her clit. "You know," he said, "if you come, everyone will see. And hear, probably, since you don't climax quietly."

Kathy was almost overwhelmed by the sensations. Bill's finger rubbed her clit, and the bread stick stroked the walls of her hot passage.

"Unzip my pants," Bill hissed, "and fuck my prick with your hand."

Unable to resist, Kathy did as he instructed. She held his rigid cock, sliding her hand up and down the long, thick shaft.

"Look over there," Bill said, indicating the two employees, now watching the activities with undisguised pleasure. "They can see what we're doing. They know."

As she rubbed, Kathy watched the waiter, hidden from the view of any of the other patrons, unzip his pants and take out his cock. "Look," Bill said. "He's jacking off. I bet he's imagining it's your hand." Soon the pressure became too much, and he hissed, "I'm going to fill your hand with my come, baby." And he did.

Then, only a moment later, as she watched the waiter climax, Kathy came, biting her tongue to keep from crying out.

After a few minutes of silence, Bill rezipped his pants and removed the bread stick from Kathy's pussy. As Kathy rearranged her clothing and put her underwear into her purse, the waiter reappeared. "Thank you, sir," he said, placing Bill's twenty-dollar bill on the table. "Thank you very much for the entertainment."

"Thank my wife," Bill said. "She's my inspiration."

The waiter looked at Kathy. "And mine." He winked, then walked back to the bar.

Bill looked at his watch. "It has been an hour, so you have paid off your wager."

"Funny," Kathy said, smiling, "I thought the bet was for two hours."

Bill grinned. "Maybe it was at that."

# *Music*

CHOPIN FILLED her head. It flowed over her like water. No, not like water, like lava. She stood in the middle of the room full of people, but, as she looked around, they faded away. They disappeared. What was going on? For an instant she was afraid, then the lava warmth filled her and she didn't care where all the people had gone. She didn't even care what was going on.

AS MARCUS WATCHED, Diana's eyes glazed over, exactly the way he had known they would. "You see, gentlemen, now the music controls her exactly the way I explained." It had taken several months of training, using drugs and hypnosis, but now Diana's body was under his complete control. He watched her as she swayed slightly in time with the music, her deep brown eyes seeing nothing, her long, dark blonde hair brushing her shoulders as she moved. Her hands were completely relaxed at her sides. As he watched, her head fell back and her eyes closed.

"Tell me how this all works," one of the men in the group asked. There were seven men, all in their late twenties or early thirties, all in full dress, standing around in the elegant living room.

"I'm afraid that's my little secret. Just let me say that Diana is at all times completely normal, charming, and intelligent, except when this music is playing. I've used the sound system here, or earphones with a Walkman clipped to her belt."

"And while she's—" the man motioned to Diana, softly swaying and seemingly in another world "—like this, she's . . . suggestible?"

"Completely. Right now she's tuned to my voice. She cannot see any of you, or hear you, unless I specifically tell her she can. I can tell her to do anything, and she'll do it. Anything. And when she awakens, that is, when the music stops, she'll remember nothing, unless I tell her to."

"Amazing."

"Remarkable."

"Is she broken in?" one man asked.

"No. Not at all. I thought whoever purchases her would like the privilege of training her."

"Hmm. Yes. That's fine. Did she agree to all of this from the beginning?"

"Yes, actually, she did. I placed an ad for a woman who wanted to be kept in luxury and wouldn't mind doing anything legal to attain that. I got hundreds of applicants, and after extensive interviews, I selected Diana and three others. Their training will be complete within a few weeks, but Diana was a perfect subject and far surpassed my expectations."

"Bring her back. I want to see how she awakens."

"Of course." Marcus walked to the CD player and changed from Chopin to Frank Sinatra.

THE CLASSICAL MUSIC was gone, and the people reappeared. Strange, Diana thought, that people should be able to appear and disappear. Oh well. She turned to the tall man who stood beside her. Hamilton. That's his name. She looked to her other side. Marcus. Yes. She had known him quite a while, but Hamilton she had met just this evening. She wondered whether this all had to do with her assignment.

Marcus had told her that she would live like a queen as long as she agreed to be her benefactor's sexual object for the occasional evening. She'd never had anything, and this was her golden opportunity. And she loved good sex. Why not get what she wanted in exchange for it.

"Mr. Hamilton," she said softly. "I'm afraid I drifted away there for a moment. What were we saying?"

"I was telling you how lovely you are."

Diana smiled ingenuously. "How could I have forgotten something so delightful? And from a man who obviously has such good taste."

Hamilton and all the other men in the room roared. "My dear," Marcus said, "you're enchanting."

Then the music played again, and she drifted away.


"MARCUS, SHE'S WONDERFUL," Hamilton said as Marcus returned from changing the CD on the stereo. "I want her."

"And so do others of us," one of the other men said. "But we'd like to see how suggestible she is."

"Of course." Marcus turned to Diana, who was obviously a million miles away, and said, "Darling. Don't you think it's warm in here?"

"I hadn't noticed it until you said it, but it is quite warm," she said, her eyes still unfocused.

"Marcus," Hamilton said, "I'd like her to be more with it. You know, I don't want a zombie."

"Diana, love, when I count to three you'll feel quite right, alive, and awake, yet you'll still hear the music and still respond to my voice and only my voice. Do you understand?"

"Yes," she said.

"One, two, three." Diana's head came up and she appeared to be completely normal. "Can you hear me?"

"Of course," Diana said.

Marcus nodded to Hamilton, who said, "And me? Can you hear me?"

Diana said nothing, nor did she indicate in any way that she heard anything. "Miraculous," Hamilton said.

"Diana, remember we were talking about how warm it is in here."

"Yes, I recall. And it's getting warmer. Maybe you should turn down the thermostat."

"Maybe you should take off the top of your dress instead."


DIANA HEARD THE MUSIC, felt the music throughout her. And she felt the lava flow through her veins, making her so warm. Small beads of perspiration formed on her upper lip and between her breasts. Take off the top of her dress. Good idea. Marcus always had such good ideas. She reached behind her, unzipped the top of her dress, and lowered it to her waist. "That's much better," she said.


THE MEN GAZED at Diana's large breasts, filling the wispy cups of her filmy lace bra. Her cleavage was deep and dark, inviting hands and mouths.

"Does that cool you off?" Marcus asked.

"Oh yes."

"Actually, it doesn't. You're still overly warm. I'll bet it's that bra. It's so hot. It's making your breasts burn and your nipples become so tightly erect." As the men watched, Diana's nipples contracted and stretched the front of the bra cups. "You need to take it off, you know."

"Of course I do," Diana said, and quickly unhooked the front clasp and removed the bra.

There was a collective sigh as the girl's magnificent breasts were revealed. Large, tipped with dark pink nipples, the breasts needed to be touched, the nipples sucked. "Who wants to play?" Marcus asked.

"I'll venture to say that we all do," Hamilton said. "She's gorgeous."

Marcus indicated Hamilton and another man, named Jacob. "Diana, your nipples are so warm, and they need something to cool them off. You can see the two men here with me, can't you?"

"Of course. They're very handsome."

The two men beamed. "They would like to help you. They have soft, wet tongues that might cool your breasts. Let them try."

Diana lifted her breasts with her hands and offered the nipples to the two men. "You have to ask them to help," Marcus said.

"Please. If you lick my nipples, I'm sure they will feel so much better."

The two men bent and licked her nipples. "That feels so good, Diana," Marcus continued. "It makes you feel so sexy. The heat you were feeling is erotic now, and it's flowing into your pussy. You can feel the heat making your pussy lips swell. Soon it's going to be hard not to invite these nice men to cool that fire also."

As all the men watched, Diana's hips started to move, and her hands fisted and unclenched. "You want to relieve that hunger, don't you? You want to touch your pussy, rub it to relieve the heat. But you can't."

"I want to," Diana said. "But I can't. What can I do?"

"Take off your dress and these two men will try to help you." Diana unzipped her dress, and it dropped at her feet. "Now your panties." Her wispy lace bikinis joined her dress on the floor at her feet. "Now sit here," Marcus said, walking over and patting the top of the bar at the side of the room.

Quickly, Diana, now dressed in only her lace-topped stockings and high-heeled shoes, lifted herself onto the bar. "It's very cool," she said.

"It's warming up very quickly from the heat of your pussy. Spread your legs so the heat can escape."

Diana spread her legs and the men all saw that her pussy was completely clean shaven. Her lips were swollen, and everyone could see how wet she was. "I have an idea," Marcus said. He moved Diana so that she was lying on the wooden surface, her spread legs toward the corners of the bar. "Now, what you want, Diana," Marcus said, "is for someone to play with your pussy. You want that very much. You also need a hard cock in your mouth, and one in each hand."

"My God, Marcus, can you have her do all that?"

"As long as the music plays, she'll do anything I want her to."

It took only a moment before Diana's body was completely occupied by the men. Hamilton was fingering her pussy. "I don't want you to put your cock into her," Marcus said. "That privilege is reserved for whoever buys her. But you can play to your heart's content."

It was only a moment before the two men whose cocks she held and the one whose erection was deeply lodged in her mouth climaxed violently. "Hamilton, would you like to come in her mouth?"

"Only when she's climaxed. Can she do that?"

"Of course. She's only waiting for my command. But maybe I should let you do that." When Hamilton smiled, Marcus said, "Diana, I want you to listen to this voice." To Hamilton, he said, "Talk to her. Tell her your name."

"My name's Hamilton, and I want you."

"His voice is as powerful as mine. You will listen to him the same way you listen to me."

As Marcus talked, Hamilton continued to play with Diana's pussy, rubbing her clit and fucking her with his fingers. "Diana," he said, "my playing with you is getting you so excited. You need to climax, but you can't just from what I'm doing. You need my mouth to make it complete."

"Please," Diana said. "Put your mouth on me. Let me come. I need it."

Hamilton grinned. "This is amazing." He leaned over and placed his mouth against Diana's swollen, naked flesh. The men could all see his tongue lapping at her juices. "Soon, Diana," Marcus said.

"Just a few more licks," Hamilton said. "You can come when I count to three. One . . ." He pressed the flat of his tongue against her clit and stroked. "Two . . ." He inserted the tip into her pussy and pushed it inside. "And . . ." he inserted two fingers in her hole and sucked her clit into his mouth, ". . . three."

Diana's body convulsed, great waves of pleasure crashing through her. Quickly, Hamilton moved around her body and pushed his erect cock into her mouth. Two men chuckled. "He won't even last until three. One, two. . ."

Before any of the men could get to three, Hamilton groaned as his hips convulsed.

Several minutes later, the men sat around the room alone.

Diana had gone to her room to get cleaned up. "Now, how much," Hamilton said.

"Fifty thousand," Marcus said.

"And she'll want for nothing. You know that I can afford to treat her like a queen."

"Of course. I wouldn't have it any other way. She's yours," Marcus said.

"What about us?" one man said.

"I really did promise Hamilton," Marcus said. "However, I've got several more women, just as wonderful as Diana, who are finishing their training. They will be ready within the month. This evening is just a sample."

"I can't wait," several of the men said.

# A Love Potion

WENDY WATCHED her husband, Matt, mix the oils. A love potion, he had told her. Was she willing to give it a try? he'd asked. Yes, she had answered. Now he was using a mortar and pestle to grind the herbs he would mix with the oils, then spread onto her body.

"God, this whole thing makes me hot," she said.

"I know," Matt said, "me, too."

"Tell me again," she said.

"Barry bought these herbs and oils in South America— some for him and his wife and some for us. He said the man told him that mixed in the proper proportions, and applied according to directions, it would make you hungrier than you have ever been. And it should work on me as well."

Wendy had heard the story several times already, and every time she listened, it made her pussy twitch and swell, becoming wet with flowing fluids. Willing? She couldn't wait. She had never been repressed nor had Matt, but their sex life had become a bit predictable over the last few months. Something new and hot would be just the thing.

Matt reread the instructions yet again and poured some of the ground herbs into a small spoon. Then he mixed them into the oil mixture. "Are you ready?" he asked, lifting his head and nodding. "This stuff is as ready as it will ever be."

"I guess I'm ready," Wendy said.

"Okay, lie down."

Naked, Wendy stretched out on their king-size bed, her head on a pillow, her legs spread.

"I have to do this as the directions say," he said, taking a hank of soft nylon rope from a brown paper bag. With an X-Acto knife he cut it into four lengths. Slowly, he lifted his wife's right wrist and tied one end of the rope around it gently but firmly. Holding the far end, he said, "Pull. I want to make sure you can't get loose."

"Is this really necessary?" Wendy asked, making what they both knew were token protests.

"According to directions," Matt answered. "If we're going to find out whether this works, we have to follow instructions."

Wendy wiggled her rope-tied wrist. The rope wasn't tied tightly enough to cause any discomfort, but Matt's knot was secure. "Great," he said, then, as she watched, Matt tied the rope to one corner post of the headboard. He quickly did the same to her other wrist.

"Why are we doing this again?" Wendy asked, yearning to hear once more how helpless she was going to be.

"The instructions say the oil must be applied to the exact spots indicated. So just in case you wiggle and cause me to get this where it's not intended," he explained, "it suggests that you be secured to the bed."

Intent on his task, Matt tied his wife's left ankle to the leg of the bed, then rounded the footboard and grasped her other ankle. He gently widened Wendy's spread legs until they were as far apart as possible without causing her discomfort. He quickly secured her right leg to the bed frame.

Wendy lay, trying to remain calm. She wanted to rip

Matt's clothes off, grab his cock, and plunge it into her, but she couldn't. She was helpless. And so hungry that she could feel her juices trickle down between her ass cheeks.

"It suggests that I make sure this isn't going to irritate, so I want to test a bit of it on your arm," Matt said. "I don't want to risk any allergic reaction or anything like that." He dipped his finger into the oil/herb mixture and rubbed a bit onto Wendy's forearm. For a full minute he stared at the slick spot in silence. "Any itching, tingling, pain? Anything unusual?"

"Nope," Wendy said, her body calming a bit as she became accustomed to the restraints. "I don't feel a thing."

"Good. Shall we go on?"

Wendy tried not to grin too widely. "I'm as ready as I can be."

Matt again dipped his finger into the oil, gazed at his wife's mouth, then rubbed a bit on her lower lip. "That should begin to feel warm in a moment." He picked up the handwritten instructions and reread a section that Wendy thought he should have memorized by now. Spread liberally on erogenous areas, it said. Begin with the lips.

As she watched Matt she felt her lower lip get warm. To cool it, she flicked the tip of her tongue over the oil. It tasted green, like the smell of new plants in the spring. How could a taste be like a smell? Her tongue tingled. "Umm," she purred. "This feels nice. Warm and tingly."

"Really?" Matt said. "More?"

"Umm, yes."

Matt spread oil on her upper lip. Again Wendy waited a moment, then felt a warm, liquid feeling. She licked her lips and rubbed her tongue around the inside of her mouth. "Nice."

Matt grinned. Neither of them had expected this to do anything. Barry was an awful practical joker and this would be just like something he would think of. "You feel something?"

"It's hard to know whether it's the stuff or just being tied like this, but I feel very excited and very relaxed at the same time."

"Hmm," Matt said. He dipped his finger into the oil and spread a thick coating on Wendy's right nipple. Immediately she felt a tightening, and the tip became almost painfully erect. "Wow," Matt said. "Maybe this stuff works after all." He spread some on her left nipple, and Wendy watched as his eyes never left her breasts.

"Taste some," Wendy suggested.

"Good idea." He leaned over and licked the tightened nub.

Shafts of electricity speared through her. Was she really hotter than she usually was? She couldn't tell. As he licked and suckled, she wiggled against the bonds that held her immobile. She wanted, needed.

He spread more oil on her other nipple and repeated the combination of licking and sucking. It was as though there was a hot wire connecting her breasts to her clit. Her juices were flowing, and she could feel her body swell and open. "I want you so much," she moaned, struggling to get her hands free so she could grab her husband.

"Not so fast," Matt said. "We really need to test this." He covered one finger with the green goo and, with slow, deliberate motions, covered Wendy's clit with it.

"Oh God," she groaned. "That's making me crazy." It was as though all of her body had ceased to exist. The only functioning area lay between her legs. She was so hot, yet powerless to grab what she wanted.

His eyes never leaving the oily flesh between his wife's legs, Matt stood and slowly began to remove his clothes. To Wendy, it seemed to take forever as he unbuckled his belt and unzipped his pants. It took hours for him to remove his jeans and shirt, then long minutes for him to slowly pull down his shorts. "I want to know how it feels for myself," he said.

"Don't waste time," Wendy moaned. "Just fuck me."

"You're so impatient," Matt said with a grin. "I want to take my time and experience all the effects." He knelt between his wife's spread legs and rubbed the tip of his cock in the oil on her nipple. "Hmm," he said. "You're right. It does feel warm."

Wendy thought she would come just from the stimulation of his cock on her nipple, but as she clenched her muscles and reached for orgasm, it eluded her.

"Maybe I need some of this all over my cock," Matt said. He pressed his shaft against Wendy's clit and rubbed the length of it against her.

Wendy was almost incoherent with lust. She burned for him as she never had before. "This oil is making me crazy. I need you so much."

Wendy watched Matt's face as he smiled, then nodded. "I need you, too," he said, sliding his cock into his wife's soaking cunt. He pulled back, then rammed it home again and again.

Wendy was in heaven, her cunt filled, her hips driving. When Matt pinched her left nipple she came, hard and fast, spasms rolling through her body, curling her toes and echoing through her. It seemed as if she had been climaxing for hours when she heard Matt's yell as he erupted within her. He collapsed on top of his wife and together they dozed.


ACROSS TOWN, Matt's friend Barry lay next to his wife, Jan. "I wonder whether Matt and Wendy have tried the love potion yet," she said.

"If I know Matt they have," Barry said. "That should be the end of their boring sex life."

"I didn't say that. Wendy had only complained that their sex had been getting a bit . . ."

"Boring."

"Ordinary."

Barry patted his wife's naked hip. "Well, ours is never ordinary."

Jan reached onto the bed table and wet three fingers with a green oily mixture. "Not a bit. You've got such an adventurous spirit. And this love potion is *sooo* fantastic." She spread it on Barry's swelling cock. "You know, we're running low. Do you think you'll be able to get more?" She fingered some onto her pussy lips.

It was all Barry could do not to giggle. Sure, he thought. All I have to do is get more of that heated massage oil and open a few herbal tea bags. "I should be able to," he whispered, sliding his cock into his wife's waiting pussy. The power of the mind is amazing, he thought. And with just a bit of help from his creative imagination . . . "I'm sure I can get as much as we want. And I understand there's a love-slave potion, too. Could I convince you to try it?"

Feeling Barry's cock fill her, she groaned, "Anything you like."

# Coming-Out
# Party

IT HAPPENED one weekend several months ago, and I must admit that I didn't even see it coming, so to speak. Let me tell you about it.

I had been feeling particularly daring that evening and so I had worn the slip dress that I had sworn I'd never wear except with my boyfriend. Well, my boyfriend was history, and I had finally realized that I wasn't. It pains me to think of the time I wasted. For almost three months after he left, I sat in the house and mourned for what had been. Well, that night I realized that enough was enough. I was alive now. Alive and horny.

I was then, and still am, an overly sexual person who needs regular sex. I had been without it for those three months, and suddenly I decided that Marge's party was just the place to get back into the swing of things. Now I've never been into one-night stands, but a quick, impersonal fling, I decided, would be just the thing to help me back into life. I took a long bubble bath, spent time on my make-up, and dressed in a lacy thong panty and blue stockings with lacy elastic tops. I put on the slip dress over my bare breasts and gazed at myself in my full-length mirror. I'm almost five eight, with a great figure, full breasts with prominent nipples, a slender waist, and a flat stomach. I turned and saw my tight ass beneath the medium blue, form-fitting silk. Not bad, I thought. I fluffed out my short auburn hair and slipped on my gold strappy, high-heeled sandals.

Ready or not, here I come.

The party was in full swing when I arrived, maybe three dozen people crowding Marge's large apartment. Men and women, drinks in hand, talked, laughed, flirted, and generally enjoyed themselves. I circulated, answered a few questions about my ex, and finally made my way to the bar. At my request, the bartender made me an extra-spicy Bloody Mary with two stalks of celery. As I wandered away from the bar, I caught the eye of a gorgeous guy, shaggy blond hair, horn-rimmed glasses, and a great smile. He raised his glass and saluted me with it. I smiled and raised mine and we drank together, our eyes locked across the room. He suggestively licked the rim of his glass so, the devil on my shoulder, I took a piece of celery from my drink and slowly inserted the end into my mouth, making a great show of licking the tomato juice from the tip.

His grin widened. He walked toward me, his eyes never leaving mine. "Hello," he said, his voice like warm velvet. "My name's Josh."

"Alicia," I purred.

We spent several minutes exchanging inanities, then we got fresh drinks and he took my elbow and led me toward a quieter spot in the hallway. "You're quite something," he said. "I know I should be suave and make light conversation, but I have to confess. All I can think about is how much I want you." He gazed openly at my breasts, and I knew he could see my nipples harden at the thought of his body loving mine.

I looked down at the front of his beige slacks. The fabric

was stretched almost to its limits. "Yes," I purred. "I can tell."

In a flash, Josh reached behind me and opened the door to a small bathroom. Quickly we were inside and the door was shut. Josh flipped on the light and pressed the small button to lock the door. Our glasses were on the floor and his arms were around me, his mouth hot and demanding. He kept repositioning his head, deepening the kiss, devouring my mouth. His tongue plunged and backed, driving, pressing. His hands tangled in my hair, and he pulled my head back. His teeth nipped a path down my neck, and his tongue licked the hollow at the base of my throat. "God," he growled. "You're amazing."

I grabbed the back of his shirt and pulled it from his waistband. My fingers found his naked skin, and I scraped my nails down his spine. "So are you," I said, my voice hoarse, my breathing rapid. I pressed my body against his, my mouth dueling with his to further deepen the kiss. I couldn't get close enough. I dragged his jacket from his shoulders, and soon it was on the floor, along with his shirt.

He was panting as though he'd just run a marathon. His teeth found my ear, and he bit, first softly and, when I encouraged him, with a gasp, hard, causing shards of both pain and pleasure to knife through me. It was animal lust, pure and simple, and it wasn't going to be satisfied easily. But we were ready.

His hands found my tits then and his long slender fingers kneaded my hungry flesh. "Too many clothes," I growled and soon his pants and shorts joined his jacket and shirt in a heap on the white tile floor. I waited and let him grab the sides of the dress and whisk it off over my head. My panties fell on top of his clothes. "Leave the stockings and shoes. That's so sexy."

His hands were everywhere, pinching, stroking, scratching. His mouth covered my shoulders with kisses, then his lips were on my breasts, and I couldn't think, just feel. I was getting soaked, and my knees would barely hold me up as he suckled.

"Turn around, grab the edge of the sink, and hold on. Tight," he said. "We're going for a fast ride."

I needed it as quickly as he did, so I turned. My hands found the edge of the ceramic sink, and I hung on. I heard him fumble for a condom and was glad he was taking care of things. Then I felt one of his hands in the small of my back, the other in my hair. "Open your eyes and watch."

I hadn't been aware that my eyes were closed, but when I opened them I looked into the mirror over the sink. The woman who looked back at me was a tiger, hair wild, mouth open, red marks on her neck and chest. I looked up and saw that Josh was as crazed as I was. "Now see how I take you," he said.

His hands grasped my hips and his hard cock found my slippery opening. He drove into me, his balls pounding against the insides of my thighs. Reap the whirlwind, I thought, and surely a tornado was whirling through my body and my soul. His hand found my clit, and he rubbed. His teeth were on my neck, his fingers pinching my nipple.

I came. Although I tried to muffle my screams against my arm, his roar drowned out any sound I might have made.

It was several long minutes before either of us moved. Then, in silence, both of us overwhelmed by the intensity of what had just occurred, we cleaned up and dressed.

Well, that was six months ago, and Josh and I are still together. We have a lot in common and we're never bored with each other, in or out of the bedroom. Is the sex always as cataclysmic as that first evening? Not always, but sometimes it overwhelms us both, and it's just two animals, fucking. At other times, it's long and gentle, and still others, it's playful or powerful.

I've got to go now. Josh's coming home early this afternoon, so I took the afternoon off from work. I'm wearing that same blue slip dress, and I've cleaned the bathroom. God, I love good, hot sex.

# Cleopatra's Treasure

"OH JOHN, it's fantastic," Lynn said, lifting the heavy necklace from its box. She held the heavy golden collar in her hand, amazed at the weight.

"It's only costume jewelry, of course," John said. "I wish it could be real."

"If it were real, it would be worth a fortune," Lynn exclaimed, "and I'd never get to wear it. Oh baby, I love it." She leaned forward and kissed her husband of fifteen years firmly on his lips. She examined the intricate bars and angles of the half-necklace/half-collar. "It's very Egyptian," she said, admiring the complex workmanship. Although not real gold, the piece had to have cost quite a bit.

"It's modeled after something Cleopatra supposedly wore," John said. "When I saw it, I naturally thought of you. I was hoping that you would dress up for me."

Lynn had a love for everything that reminded her of ancient Egypt and had quite a collection of jewelry, statuettes, and wall hangings. She also had an extensive collection of costumes. And every time she dressed up, she felt the power of the Egyptian queen course through her. She and John had some of their wildest evenings when she played queen. "Wait for me here," she said, and watched the smile spread across John's face. As she turned to go into the bedroom, she heard him get comfortable on the sofa.

In the bedroom, Lynn went to the closet and pulled out a large box. She opened the lid and withdrew a black wig, an almost-transparent dress, and a pair of two-inch platform shoes. She stripped off all her clothes, put on the wig and shoes, and took ten minutes to apply heavy makeup, with dark black outlining her eyes and lifting at the corners. Then she draped the transparent fabric around her body, fastening it with a heavy golden buckle just beneath the bosom, so it covered her yet revealed the lush outlines of her form. Then she added two gold snake cuffs to her upper arms, heavy golden earrings, and the new collar John had just bought for her.

She looked at herself in the mirror. She was strong. She was queen. She was to be obeyed.

Slowly she walked from the bedroom toward the living room, toward John.

As she entered the living room, John turned and stared. "Oh, your highness," he whispered. "You're magnificent."

"And you are my servant," she said, her voice full and strong.

John slid from the sofa, got down on one knee, and bowed his head. "Yes, your highness."

She extended one foot. Her red-painted toes were clearly exposed between the straps of the platform shoes. "Worship me."

This was an old game for them, and she and John knew the rules well. While she watched, he put his hands behind his back and linked his fingers. He was not allowed the use of his hands, just his mouth. He knelt at her feet and kissed each toe, careful to pay no more attention to any single one than another. It was incredibly erotic to have him at her feet, but when she needed more she snapped her fingers and he stopped.

"Worship me," she said, extending her hands.

With his hands clasped behind his back, he kissed each of her fingers, then sucked each into his mouth swirling his tongue around the nail. He used his mouth as if each finger were a cock, sucking in, then drawing back. Over and over he drew the essence out of each one.

God, she was hot. It was like John's mouth was pulling the heat up from her depths and making it flow to her hot pussy. Her nipples swelled, pressing against the thin fabric of her gown. She needed his mouth, and it was hers to command. She snapped her fingers again. She watched as he sat back on his heels, gazing up at her.

She extended her arms at shoulder height and nodded. She saw John reach up with trembling fingers and unbuckle the clasp of her dress. As it opened, the slithery fabric slid from her shoulders and pooled at her feet, leaving her lush body exposed to his hot gaze. "Worship me," she said again.

In his kneeling position, John's mouth was at the height of his wife's nipples. Hands behind his back, he flicked his tongue over Lynn's erect nipples, his eyes on her body. "Let me touch you," he whispered.

"You know the rules. No slave can touch the queen." Her knees were trembling so much that she was barely able to stand, but concentrating on her balance kept the heat at bay just a bit. "Now do your duty."

With a sigh, he suckled, nursing on his wife's lush breasts. He kissed the full flesh, then nipped at the erect buds. He buried his face in the valley between them and felt her flesh press against his cheeks.

Finally Lynn knew that she had to sit down before she fell. "Enough," she said, then almost fell onto a dining room chair. She parted her thighs, exposing her throbbing pussy. She had to have his mouth. "Do it," she said.

John crawled to his wife's feet and dove quickly into the fragrant cunt. He lapped and sucked, tasting her juices. He was so hard he wanted to loosen his pants, but he kept his hands behind his back. He licked the length of his wife's slit, then pushed the end of his tongue into her gaping hole.

Lynn slid forward until her buttocks were barely on the edge of the chair. Then she placed one foot on each side of the seat, held her knees, and spread her legs. "God, do it."

When John flicked his tongue over her clit, she trembled and felt her wetness spread to her thighs and trickle between her cheeks onto the wooden seat. He sucked the hard nub into his mouth and nibbled at the hot flesh. She shook, unable to keep her hips still. When he rubbed his chin against her inner lips while pulling on her clit gently with his teeth, she knew she was close.

He continued, knowing exactly where to suck, how to nip, when to lick. Suddenly, she couldn't hold back anymore. Pounding waves of ecstasy drummed through her body and her slave's mouth serviced her. "Don't you dare stop," she yelled, her orgasm lasting for what seemed like hours. Finally the waves slowed. Panting, she put her feet down and pushed her husband/slave away. "You were very good," she said.

"I hope so, your highness."

He had done well, her continuing tremors testimony to his talented tongue. She would allow him his pleasure. "Are you hot?" she asked.

"Oh yes, your highness."

She wanted to give him something special. She thought for a moment about how best to relieve John's hunger. "Then get some oil." Yes, she thought, that will work perfectly. She had always wanted to watch him jerk off, and she suspected that he would enjoy performing for her. This was her opportunity and she knew that John wouldn't let things go further than he was comfortable with. Usually their sessions ended with his cock inside her or in her hand, but this time . . .

"Oil?"

"Get the cooking oil from the kitchen."

Quickly, John disappeared, then returned with a bottle of golden oil.

"Now strip," Lynn said, calmer.

John removed all his clothes and knelt before his queen with his erect cock bobbing, needing attention badly.

"Use the oil and show me how you play with that cock of yours. I want to watch you spurt. Kneel."

"But—"

"Are you disobeying?"

"No, but—"

She raised an eyebrow imperiously, and John uncapped the oil. He filled his palm with the slippery liquid, then placed his hand on his cock. "Oh God," he said, kneeling at Lynn's feet. "Do you really want me to do this?"

"Do you question your queen?"

John's head drooped, and his fist closed on his cock.

"Does that feel good, slave?"

"Oh yes, your highness."

"Rub it. Stroke it so I can watch."

His eyes closed and his hand rubbed the length of his hard shaft.

"Faster. I want to see it come."

His hands moved faster.

"Rub your balls with the other hand."

He cupped his heavy sac with his other hand and stroked. She was getting hot again, just watching her husband pleasure himself. It was so beautiful. Although she had just had a fully satisfying orgasm, she found she was getting hungry again. She reached between her legs and touched her hardening clit. "Watch me, slave, while you do that." She gently rubbed her clit while her husband, on his knees, rubbed his erect cock and stared at her hand.

Faster and faster the two pleasured themselves until, with his head thrown back, John came, streams of thick semen arching from his cock. The sight of her husband's climax pushed Lynn over the edge, and she came for a second time.

A few minutes later, both satiated, they lay side by side on their king-size bed. "That was so wonderful." Lynn sighed.

"God, yes," John said. "I've never done anything like that before. What gave you that delicious idea?"

"I've wanted to watch you for quite a while, but I never had the nerve to ask before."

"Ask? Cleopatra never asks. She demands. And if you have any other little ideas, your slave is only too willing to do your bidding."

"Demands . . . Hmm. I'll have to give that lots of thought."

# Gift Wrap

IT WAS MIDEVENING, three days after Christmas, and Pam and Rick had finally gotten their lives sufficiently organized to begin the task of cleaning up the living room. Christmas paper, ribbons, tags, and boxes were strewn everywhere, but with three boys under six and endless visits to relatives and friends, this was the first chance the young couple had had to deal with the chaos.

"Lord," Pam said, opening a large black garbage bag, "this is such a mess." She grabbed a handful of red and green paper, scrunched it into a small ball, and tossed it into the bag.

"It's those kids," Rick said. "I don't know where they get their energy and how you cope with them every day. At least I go to work. It's restful there. It would be restful in a boiler factory." He took several cardboard boxes and smashed them flat, then stuffed them into the trash bag.

"It's not usually so crazy," Pam said, giggling. "The season and all the presents and food has them totally hyped."

"At least they're asleep now," Rick said, gathering more wrapping.

"Thank heavens for small favors." Pam gathered hanks of ribbon and draped them around her neck. "I can't bear to throw all this stuff away." She picked up a bow and chuck-led as she stuck it to the back of her hand. "Look at me, I'm gift-wrapped."

Rick's heated glance warmed Pam's belly. "I think there's some of that great eggnog you made left over," he said. "Let's at least make this a bit more comfortable." While Pam continued to gather up trash, Rick poured two glasses of eggnog and laced each with a shot of rum.

When he returned to the living room and Pam took a taste, she said, "Are you trying to get me drunk? This is po-tent stuff."

"I just might be," Rick said, leering, then returning to the task of tidying up.

It took almost two hours and another glass of eggnog each for the couple to get the living room into some sem-blance of order. Now the gifts were neatly stacked, one pile for each member of the family, wrapping paper and boxes were ready for the trash, and Pam was festooned with rib-bon.

"I'll put all this out in the morning," Rick said, tying the neck of the trash bag, "but for now I'm beat."

"Me, too," Pam said as she started to remove the arcs of ribbon draped around her neck and shoulders.

"Leave that there," Rick said, "and let's go upstairs."

Enjoying the erotic glint in her husband's eye, and quite buzzed from the rum she had consumed, Pam took Rick's arm and allowed him to lead her to their bedroom. He slipped the hook on the door into the eye on the frame. "So we won't be disturbed."

"Did you have something specific in mind?" Pam asked, a look of mock innocence on her face.

"I did indeed. Now then, my Christmas present, let me unwrap you." He lifted several lengths of colorful ribbon from around her neck. Leaving a few layers of ribbon still in place, he pushed her backward onto the bed. Falling on top of his wife, Rick pressed his lips against hers softly, then, as he felt her lean into the kiss, he deepened it, probing her mouth with his tongue. "Umm," he purred. "You taste of eggnog and rum." He kissed her again.

Pam was dizzy and warm as heat slowly flowed through her body, from her lips to her breasts and her groin. As she started to wrap her arms around Rick's neck, Rick pulled back. "Actually I'd like to wrap you up a bit more tightly," he said.

That look on Rick's face usually meant that he was hatching a delightful plan. His sexual appetite was rich and varied, and his ideas always led to an evening of great love-making. "What are you plotting?" Pam said.

Rick took a piece of wide red ribbon and wrapped it around Pam's right wrist. Then he tied the end of the ribbon to the headboard, leaving little slack.

Pam was suddenly filled with fire. Once or twice before Rick had tied her up, and she had enjoyed it thoroughly. And each time it led to a night of erotic pleasure. But since the birth of Tony, now eleven months old, their times together had been few and far between. Praying that a little voice wouldn't interrupt them, Pam gazed into Rick's lust-glazed eyes.

Rick took a long piece of green and gold ribbon and tied Pam's left wrist to the headboard, then used silver ribbon to fasten her ankles to the legs of the bed so Pam's thighs were spread wide.

Pam wriggled and pulled, reveling in the feeling of being helpless. "This makes me so hot," she whispered.

"I know," Rick said. "It does the same to me. I love looking at you this way. Struggle some more."

Pam yanked on the ribbons until both of them were sure she couldn't free herself.

"All right," Rick said, gazing down at his now helpless wife, "I've always hated those old sweats of yours." He disappeared into the bathroom and returned with a pair of bright silver shears. "That's why I bought you two new pairs for Christmas." He slid one side of the scissors under the elastic at one ankle and slowly cut the sweatpants up the side to the waist. Then he walked around the bed and slit the other side as well. With one pull the pants were in his hands.

"You know, I should complain," Pam said, her breathing now ragged. "Those were my favorites."

"Too late now," Rick said. He began at the waist of her sweatshirt and cut from hem to wrist on each side. Then with two more cuts up the arms, the shirt was in two pieces in his hand. As usual, Pam was braless, and her small tight breasts were crested by large fully erect nipples. Rick knelt on the side of the bed and took one tight bud between his teeth. He sucked hard, the way he knew Pam liked, then bit the pebbled tip.

"Ow," Pam said, squirming, trying to evade Rick's mouth.

"You can't get away from me," he replied, shifting his mouth to the other nipple and biting the tip.

"Shit," Pam said.

"Shh, or you'll wake the kids," Rick said. "No noise." He bit again.

Shards of fire rocketed through Pam's body each time Rick's teeth closed on her nipple. She clamped her jaws tightly to avoid shouting. Through her teeth she hissed, "You're making me crazy."

"I know," Rick said, shifting from breast to breast. "And you're helpless to stop me."

Pam was so hot she thought she would come without being touched between her legs at all, but suddenly, Rick was gone. She could hear him in the bathroom, searching through their toy box, which was hidden in the back of a high shelf in the bathroom closet. When he returned, she gasped at what she saw in his hand. The dildo was huge, one that he had bought for her a few years before as a joke.

Quickly he cut up the sides of her underpants and pulled them off. Then he wrapped a length of gold ribbon around her waist and tied it tightly. He looped another length of ribbon over the back of it and pulled the two ends down through the crack of her butt. Leaving the ends stretched out between her legs, he held the dildo where she could see it. "I'm going to fill you up," he said, "like you've never been filled."

"I don't know," Pam said, her eyes wide as she stared at the long, thick phallus.

"I do. And you can tell me to stop if you really need to." He rubbed the tip of the flesh-colored penis through her wetness, then slowly pressed it against her opening. As he pushed, he bit her nipple again. When she jumped, he pushed the dildo in a bit deeper. Over and over he bit her nipple and pushed the huge phallus more deeply into her cunt.

Pam gasped as she felt the twin sensations. The electricity of Rick's teeth and the feel of the dildo stretching her cunt were making her crazy. "Rub me," she whispered. "Make me come. Let me come. Rub me."

Rick pulled the ends of the ribbon up between her legs, imprisoning the dildo deep inside Pam's body. Then he looped the ribbon over the front of the one around her waist and tied it off, deftly keeping the phallus tightly in place.

"Mommy," a small voice called from another room. "Can I have a drink?"

"Oh shit," Pam said, sobering immediately.

Rick wiggled the dildo. "I'll get you one," he called. Then softly he added, "And you stay right here. Think about how full you are."

Rick slipped out of the room and, as Pam wiggled, moving the dildo inside of her, she dimly heard him easily caring for the boys. The ribbon was pressed against her clit, but she couldn't quite rub it the right way to let her come. And she needed to come. The hunger flooded all of her senses, heating her not quite to boiling. She pulled at her wrists, hoping she could free one hand to touch herself and relieve the pressure, but it was no use.

After almost ten minutes of torture, Rick returned. "All done," he said. "And how have you been?"

"Oh God, help me. Touch me. I'm so near, but I can't do it myself."

Rick grinned. "I know." Slowly he refastened the door, then undressed. As he removed his shorts, Pam could see the effect that her naked body was having on her husband's cock. Hard, strong, and totally erect, it stood out from his groin. He sat beside her on the bed and held it beside her face. "This is what you want, isn't it?"

"Oh yes," Pam said. "I want you so badly."

He stroked his cock from tip to balls. "Umm," he purred. "I could come from looking at you and rubbing myself. Maybe I will."

"No," Pam hissed.

Rick went back into the bathroom and returned with a small pouch. While Pam watched, Rick reached into the fabric bag and pulled out two slender chains with clips attached. "Remember these? Remember how crazy they used to make you?"

Nipple clamps. They hadn't played with those in years. Early in their marriage, Rick had discovered how sensitive his wife's nipples were and how they seemed to control her entire sexual reaction. Pam remembered that on several occasions Rick had clipped the clothespin-like objects to her nipples, then put an oversize shirt on her and made her walk around the house. The brushing of the cloth across the clips moved them just enough to keep her bathed in lust. She had all but attacked him. Now, as hot as she already was, she could do nothing to make herself come and nothing to stop him from stoking the fire with those clamps.

Several times he snapped the clips, then slowly he attached one to her right nipple. The effect was electric. Pam could feel the flood of her juices around the dildo, still buried in her pussy. She bucked her hips trying to use the ribbon against her clit to make herself come. When Rick attached a clamp to her left nipple the effect was doubled. Tripled. Multiplied by a hundred. She couldn't hold still. She alternately arched her back and raised her hips, reaching for something she couldn't get.

"Open," Rick said, tapping her mouth with his cock. "Do it."

She gladly opened her mouth and took all of his hard cock inside. She flicked her tongue over the tip, then licked the length of his shaft. She sucked it in slowly, then pulled her head back, creating the suction she knew he liked. Faster and faster she worked on his shaft until she could feel his orgasm build. "I can't touch your balls," she said, "so you do it. I want your hands to help me make you come."

Rick slid one hand around the base of his cock and stroked his balls. It took only a moment until Pam felt spurts of hot come fill her mouth. Unable to swallow it all, she felt some of the thick fluid dribble from the corner of her mouth.

"Oh baby," Rick whispered. "That's so good."

Moments later, Rick was between Pam's legs, twisting the dildo, then moving the ribbon so he could take her throbbing clit into his mouth. He sucked and nibbled until, in only seconds, Pam came, waves of orgasm overwhelming her, taking her breath.

It took several minutes before either of them could speak. Panting, Pam finally said, "That was the best Christmas present I've gotten in years."

Rick used the scissors to cut the lengths of ribbon from Pam's body. "Well, I certainly enjoyed wrapping it."

# Just a Guy
# and a Girl

Y OU'LL NEVER FIT the car into that space," Jena said to her husband.

"Come on, there's lots of room. I could get two cars into that." Walt pulled their Ford up next to the Toyota in front of the tiny empty space at the curb.

"Never."

"Put your money where your mouth is," Walt said.

"Okay," Jena said, a gleam in her eye. "But no money. You've got three passes to get the car into the space. If you can do it, and I'm sure you can't, you get me for an hour of servitude. And if you don't park it properly, within a foot of the curb, I get you. For an hour. Whatever I want to do. Bet?"

"Bet." Walt shifted the car into reverse, backed up and cut the wheel. After three passes, he shifted into park and said, "Okay. Done."

Jena opened her door and looked at the curb. "It's not parked, it's abandoned. It's at least a mile from the curb."

Walt got out and, much to his dismay, even he had to admit it was at least two feet away. "Hmm. How about one of Shaq's feet?"

"Not a chance. So now you're mine. Tonight. For one

hour." Jena grinned, then got out of the car, and Walt watched his wife disappear into the crowd.

That evening, they put the children to bed, went into the bedroom, and Jena locked the door. "Okay, baby, now you belong to me for one entire hour." She placed the oven timer she had brought with her on the dresser and set it for the required time. "Now," she snapped, "strip. We're going to play a game."

Jena had given the evening a lot of thought. She had a good idea of her husband's deepest fantasy, and tonight she was going to make it come true. She also knew that he would stop her if she went too far. They trusted each other completely.

Walt looked at his wife and grinned. Their sex life had always been adventurous and creative. As he pulled his T-shirt off over his head, he wondered exactly what she had in mind. Never mind, he told himself. It would undoubtedly be fantastic. He slipped off his shoes and removed his socks. Then he opened his jeans and pulled them and his shorts off. Naked, his erection hard and sticking straight out from his groin, he stood, watching his wife's eyes roam over his body.

"Tonight, we are going to change roles. You're going to become a girl, and I'll be the guy. You get to go first. I'm going to change you into a beautiful woman."

"Hey now, wait a minute," Walt said.

To Jena's ear, his protests were not quite convincing. Over the years of their marriage, Jena had watched her husband go from mildly curious to wildly fascinated with women's apparel and makeup. He loved to watch her put on her eyeliner, foundation, blush, and lipstick. Often he would sit on the bed as they prepared to go out, his eyes never leaving her legs as she put on her stockings. So now, she was going to give him the full treatment. "No, you wait

a minute. Are you welching? We had a bet, you remember."
She looked at his cock, sticking straight out from his groin.
"You can't lie to me. You're excited, and you're going to be
more so as I create the new you."

"Yeah, but—"

Jena stared at her husband and raised a questioning eyebrow. His mouth closed, and he rested his hands in his lap.
Jena rummaged in her bureau drawer and found an old,
stretched-out pair of panty hose. She took a pair of scissors
and cut a hole in the front. "Now put these on."

Walt was slight, of slender build, so Jena knew the hose
would go on with only a bit of difficulty. She watched as
Walt held the stocking in his hand, staring at the flesh-
colored nylon. She watched the indecision wash over his
face, then she saw him make up his mind. He sat down on
the bed and stuck his toe into the right stocking leg.

"Not that way," Jena said. "You've seen me do that lots of
times. Like this." She knelt at his feet and scrunched the
right panty hose leg onto her thumbs. Then she nodded
and Walt stuck his toe into the opening. Slowly Jena drew
the tight nylon up his leg, to just above the knee. Then she
repeated the process with his other leg. "Stand up." As she
pulled the hose up the rest of the way she watched as his
cock twitched and pre-come leaked from the tip. She had
been right. This was driving him crazy.

"You know," she said as she stepped back to look at her
handiwork, "for next time, I'll have to get some other things
for you to wear. Maybe a large bra. You'd look so wonderful." Her mind racing, she finally thought of a pair of baby-
doll pajamas that she hadn't worn in several years. While
Walt watched her every move, she found them in her closet
and held the top out for him to see. "For tonight, we can
put this on you."

Walt was silent and immobile, obviously unable to control his body. "Arms up," Jena said and slowly Walt's arms lifted. She slipped the white nylon pajama top over his hands, down his arms, and over his head until the straps were on his shoulders and the floaty fabric covered his chest. Jena stroked her husband's belly, shoulders, and back through the smooth material, noting his breathing quicken, his hands tremble. "Mmm," she crooned, "so smooth. So soft."

"Oh Lord," Walt groaned. "Oh Lord."

Jena glanced at the timer. She still had about half an hour. They spent the next fifteen minutes in the master bathroom as Jena used all her makeup to create a woman's face on her husband's body. "Beautiful," she said finally.

"Oh baby."

"Now we need to complete this sexual swap. Go inside and wait for me." She closed the bathroom door and sighed. About two months earlier she had ordered several sex toys from a catalog and, for some reason, she had ordered a harness and a selection of dildos. She had put them into her toy bag in the bathroom closet and left them there. Had she known this evening was coming?

Now she quickly stripped. Her nipples were hard, her pussy soaked. This entire situation was making her incredibly hot. She fit a slender dildo into the harness's opening and slid a second, heavier dildo into her sopping pussy. "Very clever," she muttered as she fit the rest of the harness on, fastening heavy leather straps around her hips and pressing the base of the artificial penis against her clit. She could feel the throb of her excitement as her clit was stimulated and the thicker dildo filled her cunt, held in place by the harness straps. A slender rod now stuck out from her groin. She took a deep breath, opened the bathroom door, and stepped out.

Walt had been staring at the door and now just sat, unmoving, his eyes wide, his breathing so loud she could hear it across the room.

"My lovely girl needs a good fucking," Jena said.

Slowly and silently, Walt rose to his feet.

"Bend over," Jena said, walking up to him. She turned him around and pushed him so he was bent over the bed, his ass in the air. She took the scissors and snipped a hole in the rear of the panty hose. "Now, my sweet girlie, you will get a good fucking." She grabbed a tube of lubricant from her bedside table and applied a large dollop to the dildo. "But I must be sure my girlie is ready." She put another big dollop on her hands and rubbed it around his asshole, penetrating only a half inch. Her penis would do the rest of the job quite well. The dildo in her pussy made her knees shake, and she knew that with just a few thrusts the clit stimulator would make her come.

Slowly, Jena pressed the tip of the slender dildo against Walt's opening and pushed.

"Oh no," Walt said as the rod penetrated his virgin rear. "Oh no." But to Jena's ears, the sound was not a negation, but an affirmation. And she knew that he would use their safe word if he really wanted her to stop.

"Oh yes, girlie," Jena said. "Oh yes. You need a good fucking." She pushed gently but steadily, and inexorably the dildo penetrated Walt's rear. As she pushed, her clit rubbed against the plastic clit tickler, and the dildo moved inside her cunt. She pulled back, then pushed, simulating fucking. In and out as the sensations in her pussy drove her higher.

Her hand still slippery from the lubricant, Jena reached around and grabbed Walt's cock. Shaking with impending orgasm, she rubbed. "Baby," Walt yelled as his cock erupted, spilling gobs of hot semen on the bed. Jena kept thrusting as the clit stimulator rubbed and she felt the orgasm explode in her belly. "Yesss," she hissed. "Yesssss." The orgasm went on and on, then finally calmed.

She pulled out, and the two lovers collapsed onto the bed, panting.

Later, they showered together and climbed between cool sheets. "I'm not gay," Walt said.

"Of course you aren't," Jena said. "That was just fun to play with, just you and me."

"Just you and me?" Walt said.

"Right. Just a guy and a girl indulging in good sex together."

"Yeah," Walt said, grinning. "Just a guy and a girl." They cuddled together and fell asleep.

# Tennis

I THINK it was her legs that got me. I love strong, well-developed legs, and as I watched her about to serve at forty-fifteen, I knew I was in love. No, actually I was in lust. I sat down at a small table beside the court and put my gin and tonic on the table in front of me.

As I knew she would, she tossed the ball, then raised her racket over her head, prepared to swing. Her breasts pressed against the stretchy fabric of her shirt, and I was sure I could see the large nipples outlined against the material. She swung and I was in heaven. So I sat, waiting for my friend Jack to join me for singles, and just stared. I propped my chin on my hand and closed my eyes, imagining she was mine.

SUDDENLY, we were alone on the court and it was twilight. "What's your pleasure?" she asked, her voice husky and deep. She was still wearing the white knit shirt and short tennis skirt.

"You are," I said. "Come here." She did, and I pressed her against my now hard cock. God, I wanted her so badly. I looked at her mouth, soft, warm, slightly open, then pressed my lips against it, teasing, tasting. I licked her lips and watched her head fall back. I ran my tongue over the pulse in her throat, then blew on the wet trail, enjoying her body's obvious reaction.

"You're mine tonight," I said.

"I know," she whispered.

There was a chain-link fence surrounding the court, and I slowly walked her backward until her spine pressed against the cold steel. "Feel good?"

"Oh yes," she purred.

I grabbed her wrists and stretched her arms over her head against the fence, pressing and holding her against the cold steel. I felt her hips buck and I saw her lips reach for mine. "That excites you, doesn't it?"

"Yes," she hissed, her breath whooshing out between her teeth.

There were silk scarves in my hands, and I quickly tied her wrists to the links, just tightly enough that she couldn't get away. Her eyes were hot, her mouth open. "Spread your legs," I ordered, and she stepped out as wide as she could. More scarves tied her ankles. Now she was truly mine, comfortable yet unable to move more than an inch in any direction. My cock ached to be inside of her, but I had a lot to do first.

"You're a problem, my love," I said. "You make me too hard to wait. But I have a cure for that." I unzipped my shorts and pulled out my hard-on. I wrapped my hand around it and slowly began to stroke along its length.

"No, don't do that," she moaned. "It's mine. It should be inside my pussy."

"Later," I said. "He will be deep between those gorgeous legs soon enough, but he has to have something now." I rubbed and, in only a moment, semen boiled inside of me and erupted onto the asphalt at her feet. God, it was good, and the sight of her eyes, staring at my cock, made it so much better. I wanted to sit and just enjoy the afterglow but there was going to be so much more. "Now we have some time."

A bag awaited me on the ground a few feet away, and inside I found a pair of scissors. "First," I said, "you're wearing way too many clothes." With slow precision I cut up the front of her shirt, then out through both sleeves until I could pull the shirt off. Now her almost naked back was pressed against the cold links of the fence. "How does that feel?"

"Cold." She trembled, from a combination of the cool air on her skin and her lust for me. It was as though I could read her thoughts as she looked at me with hot eyes. She wanted me. But not yet. We had a long way to go.

With one snip her sports bra parted. Two more snips, and the straps were severed and it was in my hand. I stared at her nipples, so large and fully erect, her breasts lifted as her arms remained immobile above her head. I leaned over and flicked my tongue over the deep brown tips, watching them almost reach for my mouth. "I know what you like, you know," I said. I took a pair of suckers from the bag at my feet and quickly attached them to her wet nipples. I watched her writhe and squirm with pleasure as the suction devices tugged at her overheated flesh. "Tell me."

"Hot, so hot. They feel like your mouth sucking on my tits, both at the same time. It's almost too much."

I smiled. "Almost."

She looked at me, then closed her eyes.

Next, I cut off her skirt and the attached stretchy panties until she stood revealed to me. I placed my palm against her belly and pushed, forcing her buttocks against the cold fence. She jerked and moaned, tossing her shoulder-length hair from side to side as she almost writhed with the pleasure of it.

Again I reached into the bag, and this time I withdrew a length of slender chain. I wrapped it around her waist, fastened it with a small padlock, and moved it around until the lock was in the small of her back, the remaining length of chain hanging almost to the ground, cold between her butt cheeks.

She was almost incoherent with lust, but thanks to my earlier masturbation, I could wait . . . and watch. I pulled a large dildo from the bag. "Open your eyes," I said.

Slowly her lids rose, and I held the oversize artificial penis in front of her face. "You know where this is going, don't you?"

"Oh no. That won't fit." It was bright red, probably nine inches long and more than two inches in diameter, with a ring at the blunt end.

"Yes, it will. I know how hot you are, and I know you can take it all." I bent over and rubbed the tip of the cock against her soaked pussy. As I had known it would, it slipped inside her easily, yet I knew it stretched her in the most delightful way. When it was lodged deeply within her, I pulled the hanging length of chain between her legs, threaded it through the ring, and fastened it to the chain at her navel with another small padlock. She moaned and bucked her hips, trying in vain to hump the dildo, trying to make it fuck her the way she wanted, needed.

"Now the fun begins. You know I love to tease you, baby," I said. "I love it when you're so close to coming that you beg, but you know I won't let you." I pulled a small box from the bag. "Well, I will let you, eventually."

I knew every detail of how the device worked. There was a nob that protruded from the side of the blunt end of the dildo and slowly revolved around the thick rod, rubbing against the sensitive areas just inside a woman's passage. I turned a small dial on the box. She went wild, rotating her hips, trying to get more of the dildo to move, to satisfy her lust. I listened as her body's movements made the fence clang and rattle. She was beyond caring about the noise. "Please," she moaned. "You're driving me crazy."

I smiled. There was still one more goodie, a tickler, a hidden rod that could slide from the blunt end and slowly massage a woman's clit. I pressed the lever now to activate it.

I knew she was close, but each time she was ready to drive herself over the edge, I slowed or stopped the motion of the delightful device lodged deep in her cunt. Over and over I pushed her to the brink, and each time I backed her off, until sweat was running down her body and my cock was hard again. With a tiny key I removed the lock at her navel and released the chain. I cut the scarves that held her ankles, leaving her arms pressed against the fence.

I quickly stripped and put on a condom. I wanted the freedom to do as I pleased. And I knew what I pleased. I grabbed her ankles and draped her knees over my arms so her ass hung free against the fence. She loved to be ass fucked, and I was going to finish this in my favorite way. I rubbed my covered cock in the juices that ran freely down the insides of her thighs. Then I rubbed my hard dick around the rim of her hole, and slowly pressed it into her. Ever so gradually my cock entered her rear passage, made tighter by the huge dildo still lodged inside of her. "Oh yes, baby," she cried. "Fill me up. Please, do me hard."

Hard it was. I rammed my cock up as far as it would go, then turned the two parts of the device up full. I could feel the nob as it rubbed against her passage and thus against my cock. I wanted to wait, but it was no use. With a bellow, I came again, my cock pounding into her. I reached between us, wiggled the dildo and rubbed her clit. She screamed, a long, loud noise that would have awakened the dead. "Yes, yes, yes," she cried. "Yesssssss."

"HEY BUDDY," a voice said. "Are you asleep?"

I jerked upright, my wrist sore from supporting my head. "Oh shit," I said, swiveling my head to see Jack standing above me.

"Long day?" he asked.

"I guess." Still scrambled, I tried to hold on to the vision of the woman as she came, but as with most dreams, it was already fading.

"That's game, set, and match," a voice yelled from the court. "Nice game, Terry, but not good enough yet."

"Hey, ladies," Jack yelled. "If you're not too tired, how about a set of doubles?"

"Sure," one said. The one with the breasts and the incredible legs. "My name's Terry and that's Paula. Which one of you is the better player?"

"Actually I am," Jack said, "so since you're the winner, you take Jake, and I'll play with Paula. We'll show you two how tennis is really played."

I watched all of this, the fog rapidly lifting. I grabbed my racket from the bag at my feet. Looking at the bag brought back shards of my foggy dream. Dream? Maybe. But could it happen? I ran out onto the court. "Hi. I'm Jake."

She reached out her hand. "Hi." We shook. "We can volley for serve." She winked at me. "And loser buys drinks afterward."

# The Power
# of Love

ROB AND CASSIE had been married for seven years. Although they were planning on having a family eventually, they both worked and were willing to wait.

One Saturday evening they were sitting in their living room, amazed that they had no social plans. "What would you like to do this evening?" Cassie asked. "We could see what's at the movies."

"I'd prefer to stay home and fool around all evening," Rob said, leering at his wife and twirling an imaginary mustache.

"Mmm," Cassie said, snuggling close. "Sounds good to me. How about a bubble bath?"

Rob took a deep breath and mentally crossed his fingers. "I had something different in mind."

"Oh?" Cassie looked at her husband. "You look serious. What's up?"

Again Rob filled his lungs with air and let his breath out slowly.

"Come on, babe," Cassie said. "Tell me. Is something bothering you?"

"Things have been real good in the bedroom department recently and, well . . ."

Cassie sat silently, waiting for Rob to tell her what was going on.

Finally he said, "I've had a fantasy for, well almost forever, and I'd like to play. But I don't know how to discuss it or whether you'd be interested."

"Go on," she said softly.

Rob turned so he couldn't see Cassie's face as he revealed his deepest desire. He trusted her to be honest with him, yet not hurt him as he took a risk, telling her something so difficult. "I don't think I ever told you that I got into hypnosis in high school. I got pretty good, actually."

"No, you never told me. Did you do the cluck-like-a-chicken stuff? I've always thought that was a bit much."

"No, I never embarrassed anyone like that. But I did have fun at parties with people who were willing to play." He swallowed hard and again mentally crossed his fingers. "Would you be willing to play?"

"You mean let you hypnotize me? I guess. Do you think you remember how?"

For weeks, Rob had been contemplating approaching Cassie with this idea, so he had been poring over his old books on the subject. He had even gone to a bookstore on his lunch hour to get a few new ones. He remembered everything. "Yes, I still know how, but your 'I guess' isn't good enough. I'd be interested only if you were one hundred percent willing. I'd want your complete cooperation."

Rob still faced away from his wife, but from her long silence, he could imagine Cassie thinking about what he had proposed. He had wanted to play for as long as he had had sexual fantasies. Hypnotize a woman and have her under his control. He got hard just thinking about it now. But it had to be a cooperative thing.

"It sounds exciting," Cassie said finally. "Is it true that

you can't make someone do something they don't really want to do?"

Rob turned toward his wife and looked deeply into Cassie's eyes. "Whether I can or can't, you'd have to trust me completely not to do anything you didn't want. I know you well, in and out of bed, and I just want to have some fun. I'd never do anything that you wouldn't enjoy."

Cassie smiled. "I do trust you, babe. Let's try it. What do I have to do?"

Rob sighed and grinned. "Really?" Was it really going to be this easy? Why hadn't he suggested it years ago? he wondered.

Cassie giggled. "Yes, really. This is something you really want, and the idea turns me on, actually. I would be kind of a sex slave. Kinky. Can I make one request? I've seen this stuff on TV and they sometimes make the person in the trance forget what went on. Don't make me forget what we do. Okay?"

Rob's grin widened. "Not a chance. You will remember everything and so will I." He got up and disappeared into the bedroom, then returned with a candle. He lit it, set it down on the coffee table, then turned out all the lights. "Sit comfortably and put your hands on your thighs. Just look at the candle and relax. Take a deep breath and relax."

Rob watched his wife put her hands on her legs and visibly relax. "I want you to feel the heat of the candle in your fingers," he said, his voice low and soothing. "They will feel it first, since they are close to the candle. Do you feel the heat?"

"Yes."

"Good. The heat is very relaxing. It travels up your arms and now you can also feel it in your knees and thighs. Does it feel good?"

"Yes."

"Warm and soft and comfortable."

"Yes," Cassie said, her breathing deepening.

The litany returned to him like riding a bicycle. He had done this often in high school, and now all the moves and words rushed back into his head. But this time it was also different. This time it was his wife, and he was going to do things with her that he hadn't had the nerve to do before. "That's fine. As that heat flows through your legs and arms, they get so relaxed. The heat is so relaxing. Feel it flow through your arms and legs, and now into your belly and chest. You feel almost heavy, yet totally relaxed. It's warm and comfortable, washing over you. Tell me how you feel."

"I feel good," Cassie answered, her voice thick, her breathing deep. "Relaxed and good. Warm."

"Wonderful. That's just right. Now the heat flows into your neck and face. As it flows to your eyes, they want to close because you're so relaxed. It's all right if they close. That just makes you feel more relaxed." He watched his wife's eyes slowly close. "Good. Very good. Are you feeling very relaxed?"

"Yes."

"Good. And every time you say the word *yes*, you get even more relaxed. You know you're being hypnotized, don't you?"

"Yes."

"And you are enjoying it?"

"Yes."

"Good. You feel all warm inside, and that warmth is relaxation. Now, are you willing to play with me?"

"Yes," Cassie said softly. "I want to play with you."

"Okay. You can open your eyes. And with your eyes open, you'll be even more relaxed." He watched Cassie's eyes slowly open. "I want you to be my sex kitten. Can you do that?"

"I don't know how," she said slowly.

"I will teach you. But being my sex kitten is the most wonderful thing you can think of being. Is that right?"

Cassie smiled. "Oh yes. That would be wonderful."

He had fantasized about this so often that he knew exactly what he wanted. First he had to make her feel sexy and hot. "How would a sex kitten look, do you think?"

"She'd have big tits and a tiny waist. She'd have long hair all the way down her back."

"If that's how you think you should look, we will make that happen."

"We will?"

"Yes. Stand up and undress. It's comfortable for you to do that. And as you shed your clothing, you'll also shed any shyness you have. You are a sex kitten, and sex kittens aren't shy about anything."

Cassie stood up and, as Rob watched, slowly removed her shirt, jeans, shoes, and socks, then her bra and panties. She stood, gloriously naked, her shoulders back, her breasts thrust forward. She looked anything but shy. "You don't think you look like a sex kitten?"

Cassie looked down. Rob had always loved his wife's body, but he knew that she wanted her breasts to be bigger. "No."

"Come into the bedroom," he said, and she dutifully followed him. "Now look at yourself in the mirror. You are a sex kitten, but you need some special clothing." He and Cassie had bought some sexy lingerie from a catalog a while back and had had an evening of hot sex when she first wore bits of the outfit. But now it had lain in the drawer for months. He found a black waist cincher with no bra cups and a pink ribbon up the front. He wrapped it around her waist and fastened the dozen hooks up the back. "Now look at yourself," Rob said. "Amazing things will happen as I pull the ribbon tighter." He grasped the ends of the pink satin. "As I pull, your waist will get smaller and your breasts will grow. I'm going to pull just a bit now. Tell me what you see."

"Oh," Cassie gasped. "That's wonderful. My tits are so big now. And my waist is much smaller."

"I'll pull again and it will happen still more." I pulled.

"Oh." Cassie cupped her breasts and held them in her hands. "Oh."

"Now one last pull. With that one, your hair will get longer and turn deep black, too." He pulled one last time. "Then you will look just like a sex kitten."

"Oh it's so wonderful."

"Now that you're a sex kitten, I want you to kneel before me. And as your knees touch the carpet you will be even more relaxed. You will see only me, and you will believe me to be the sexiest man you've ever seen."

He watched as his wife knelt at his feet. This was his fantasy come true, and with his own wife. "Now I'm wearing some very sexy clothes, but you must remove them. They are getting in the way of your seeing me. Now take them off."

Cassie reached out and unzipped Rob's jeans. "So beautiful," she said as Rob's hard cock sprung free. Her breathing quickened as she gently touched his cock with the tip of her index finger.

"But the rest of my body is sexy, too. And as you remove each piece of my clothing, you will get more relaxed, but hotter, hungrier. First my shirt." He gradually instructed her to remove all his clothing until he was naked.

"Now kneel again, and remember that each time you

kneel down you get more deeply into that wonderful re-laxed place." She did. "Now you want nothing more than to touch my cock. Take it in your hand and stroke it." Until then he had been able to hold his excitement in check, but with his wife's hands fondling his cock and balls, he sud-denly realized that he was rapidly losing control. "Okay, stop now." He could wait.

Cassie settled back on her haunches, her hands resting on her thighs. "Now you are so hungry for me it's hard to wait. Are you wet?"

"Oh yes."

"Touch it." Cassie reached between her thighs and wig-gled her finger into her crotch. "Show me."

Cassie wet her finger and extended it so her husband could see. He licked the moisture from the tip. "Good. But we need to make it easier. You'll be much more comfortable on the bed." It took only a moment until Cassie was lying, spread-eagled. "Now touch it where it's hot." He loved to watch as Cassie occasionally masturbated while they made love, but she was usually in a hurry to feel his cock inside. In his fantasy he could watch her as long as he wanted. And this was his fantasy. "Touch it." Cassie's hand worked be-tween her legs, rubbing, making circles over her clit. "Can you come that way?"

"Yes."

"Good, do that. I want to watch you come." As he watched, Cassie's eyes closed and her fingers flew. Suddenly Rob watched her back arch and her breathing almost stop. "If you want to scream, it's all right. It will feel natural." She was always silent when she came but now, he knew, she needed the outlet.

Cassie yelled as her hands worked and her body spasmed. Rob loved it. She was so beautiful when she came. So beau-tiful. And he was so hot and his cock so hard that it almost hurt. Now he wanted to watch his wife's beautiful hands on him. He waited until her breathing slowed. "Are you calm now?" he asked.

"Yes," she said, softly.

"Well, you need to touch me now. My cock needs your hands." He knelt on the bed so she could reach him without moving. He watched her reach out ever so slowly until he felt her hands caressing his hard, erect penis. And he wanted to come. "Faster," he said, and with his encouragement she found his rhythm. He had seen come shots in XXX-rated films, and he had wanted to come on his wife's face for a long time. Now he would do it. "Yes," he whispered. "Yes." Come boiled from his balls and erupted from his cock, spurting onto his wife's beautiful cheeks. "Open your mouth," he said, and the second spray found her spread lips. "Lick it." She did, her soft pink tongue snaking out and finding the gobs of thick, white fluid. God, Rob thought, it's another of my fantasies. So good.

It was long minutes before he finally calmed. Then he wet a small towel in the bathroom and slowly washed Cassie's face. Finally he said, "Now I will tell you a word that will put you back into this trance whenever we want. Marshmallow. When I say 'marshmallow' your eyes will close and you will be back in this wonderful place where you are now. Do you understand?"

"Yes," she said, still lying on the bed.

"And when I clap my hands, you will be awake. And you will remember everything that happened." He clapped and watched the subtle changes in Cassie's body that signaled to him that she was no longer hypnotized.

"Phew," she said. "That was amazing."

"Do you remember everything?"

"I think so. I came so hard that I'm exhausted. So good. I watched you come. That was great."

"I gave you a word that will put you back there. If you want, I will remove that part, and I won't ever do this again." Rob was amazed at how disappointed he would be, but this had to be her decision.

"I loved it. It felt good. But it's our secret. No one else is ever to know."

"Absolutely."

"And if I decide I don't want to do this again, we won't. Right?"

"Right. I love you and would never do anything you didn't want."

"Good. And what was that word again?"

"Marshmallow."

Cassie smiled and sighed and closed her eyes.

# A Shower Massager

PHIL ARRIVED at his motel late in the evening. He was beat. Seven hours of driving and then, when he'd gotten off the interstate, he'd gotten thoroughly lost. Now it was almost nine and he was hungry, tired, and very cranky.

He'd left later than he'd planned that morning. Carol had been so gorgeous, lying in bed wearing a nightgown that just drove him crazy. He'd showered and dressed, vowing this time to get an early start. But when he bent over to kiss her good-bye, she'd put his hand on her breast. Soft and firm, covered with that satiny fabric that slithered and slipped and almost flowed beneath his hand. He had felt her nipple harden, and he'd been a goner. It had taken almost two hours before both of them were satisfied.

Then another shower, breakfast, hours of driving with a drive-through burger for lunch. What a way to spend a Sunday. But he was here now, and ready for his eight o'clock meeting the following morning. Bright eyed and bushy tailed. That's what he'd be in the morning. Just a few minutes to hang up his clothes so they wouldn't look like he had slept in them, and a quick bite at the diner next door. Then a good night's sleep and he'd be ready.

He opened his suitcase and there, on top, was a small, gift-wrapped package. Inside the silver paper he found a small tape player, with a tape already inside. He pushed play and heard his wife's familiar voice.

"Hello, darling.

"I miss you so much already, and I wish you didn't have to be away from me so much of the time. This traveling you do is so hard on both of us. And what's a poor horny woman to do? You know I won't ever cheat on you, but I'm hungry. All the time. So I've learned how to handle it myself. Get it? Handle? I thought you'd enjoy my little play on words.

"With you away so much of the time, I'm developing new ways to please myself, and I thought you might want to hear about one I think will be *sooooo* good."

Phil set the player on the table beside his bed. He stretched out on the spread and crossed his ankles. Dinner could wait. After all, the diner was open twenty-four hours, and listening to his wife's sexy voice was causing him to develop a different kind of hunger.

"I'm recording this on the Wednesday of last week when you were away. Remember how we talked on the phone and almost made love through the wires that night? I came, rubbing my pussy while you stroked your cock, so far away."

Phil smiled. He remembered that evening well. They'd stayed on the phone for almost two hours and he'd gotten almost no sleep. Fortunately that meeting had gone well in spite of him.

"I know that the phone bill for that evening was so enormous that we've vowed to talk only once for each trip, and then for only a few minutes. But what good is that? How can a girl get off that way? Well, I've found other ways, and I thought you should know about a few of them.

"You know what I like best? Well, I'm going to run a big tub full of hot water and I'll be back."

Phil heard a few moments of silence, then a snap on the recorder. Then his wife's voice began again.

"Did you miss me? I filled our big bathtub with hot water, and now the recorder is sitting on the sink beside the tub. I'm in the water, all naked. I've got the soap in my hands, and I'm rubbing up a good lather. The soap is so slippery as I rub my hands over it. So slippery."

Phil could hear the sound of water sloshing. He could picture his wife's body, lush and full. No skinny women for him. Soft, curvy, with lots of flesh he could knead and stroke. He moaned low. Thinking about his wife's body was making him hard.

"I'm rubbing the lather over my breasts now," her voice continued. "All over, but I'm not touching my nipples. They are all pointed and tight because they are wet from the bathwater and cold from the chill air. But I've got the space heater blasting for what I want to do later so I'll be warm soon.

"I'm looking at my tits as I rub soap on my ribs. You love my breasts, don't you? They are very white with tan lines where my bikini ends. Dark tan, white skin and dark, hard nipples.

"I think they need my fingers now, so I'll lather my hands again. Hard, slippery soap. Remember when we made love in the tub a few weeks ago? I lathered your cock then with my soapy hands."

Phil remembered. He unzipped his jeans and rearranged his shorts so his hard cock could get some room. He remembered.

"I'm rubbing my tits now, but I wish these were your hands. Pinching my tight little buds. Swirling around my white skin. Cupping my big globes. I'm stroking my ribs and belly now with one hand, while the other is busy with my tit. God, this feels good."

Phil's breathing quickened as he listened to his wife's voice. He heard the tape being shut off, then starting again.

"Did you wonder where I went? Well, I've let most of the water out of the tub. The heater has really helped, so the room is steamy-hot. I've taken the shower massager down from the pole and I have it in my hand. I'm turning on the water. Shit," she hissed, "that's cold." There was a pause. "That's better," Carol said.

Phil grinned and opened the fly of his shorts to allow his erection to spring free.

"I'm turning the nozzle to pulse and spraying the water on my tits."

Phil could hear the water as he pictured his wife lying naked in the tub.

"God that feels so good. It's like dozens of tiny fingers playing with my nipple. I'm adjusting the spray so it's needle fine. It almost hurts my boobs, but it feels exciting. I'm getting so hot. Now, I've readjusted it to pulse. That's the best. Oh God, so good."

Phil wrapped his hand around his cock and rubbed slowly.

"Now the spray is on my belly. It sort of tickles. I want to aim the spray at my pussy, but I'm deliberately holding back. It's nice to wait, to anticipate how that pulsing water will feel on my clit, on my lips, on my asshole."

Phil's hand moved faster.

"I can't wait any longer. I'm spraying my pussy now." Phil heard a long-drawn-out sigh. "That's wonderful. Not as good as your hands or your cock or, of course my favorite, your mouth. But what's a girl to do? God, it's good. I'm going to come without actually touching my snatch. Just this wonderful water. It just keeps pulsing, kneading my flesh. God, it's good. Just a little more."

Phil listened to the small animal noises his wife was making, knowing the sounds of her orgasm. For several long minutes, all he heard from the tape player were the sounds of the water and his wife's loud moans. "Yes," she hissed finally. "Yesssssss."

Phil suddenly stopped rubbing his cock, turned off the tape player, grabbed the phone, and dialed his home number. "Hello," Carol's soft voice said.

"Hi, darling," Phil said.

He heard Carol's giggle. "You're late. I expected your call an hour ago."

"I got lost trying to find this damned . . . What do you mean, you expected my call? We had agreed to cut down on the phone calls."

"You got my tape?"

Phil's smile widened. "Yes."

"Well, I just want you to know I'm lying here on the bed, without any clothes on. Would you like to know what I'm doing? Where my hand is right now?"

Phil began to stroke his cock again. "Yes, darling, you know I'd love to."

# Stocking Stuffers

LISA FOUND the catalog in the bathroom at her friend Carrie's house one early December afternoon. "Do you really order stuff from this?" she asked when she returned to their Christmas decorating.

"Sure. We get a lot of catalogs. Rick and I paw through them, and just doing that gets us hot." She giggled. "Then we order a new toy or piece of lingerie and play again. Lord, it's fun."

"I would be so embarrassed," Lisa said.

"Yeah, we were, too, at first. But even the embarrassment is exciting." She winked at her friend. "You know, Christmas is coming. Take that catalog. You could just stuff Ted's stocking with that. Think of the possibilities."

"Hmm," Lisa said, putting the small slick-paper magazine in her purse. "Yeah. Think of that."

Later that evening, after Ted fell asleep, Lisa thumbed through the catalog, her eyes widening as she gazed at the items for sale. As she turned the pages, her pulse speeded up, her breathing quickened, and her pussy moistened. After she closed the booklet, she climbed into bed beside Ted, woke him by nibbling on his neck, then fucked him senseless.

"What was that all about?" Lisa's husband asked when he caught his breath.

"Oh, nothing. I just wanted you."

"Well, whatever caused that 'nothing,' bottle it."

"Ummm, yeah," Lisa mumbled as she fell asleep.

The following afternoon, Lisa again browsed the catalog, found three items she wanted to buy for Ted's stocking, and called the company's 800 number. Contrary to her fears, the ordering process was simple and impersonal. The items she had ordered arrived in an unmarked package a few days later, and she quickly hid them in the back of her closet.

On Christmas morning, Ted and Lisa's three children filled the house with whoops of glee as they unwrapped their treasures. There were presents from the kids to their parents, and nice, practical gifts from each parent to the other.

Throughout the day, Lisa found her thoughts wandering to the items she had carefully gift wrapped and returned to the closet for later. Fortunately for Lisa's patience, the children dropped into bed, exhausted, early that evening.

The two parents cleaned up the family room and finally went upstairs. "Honey," Lisa said, her heart pounding, "I've got a few more presents for you."

"You have?" Ted said, puzzled. "I loved the sweater, and that new fishing gear was just what I wanted."

"I'm glad you liked what I got you, but I think you'll like these, too."

"I don't have anything else for you," Ted said, looking chagrined.

"You will," Lisa said with a grin as she led Ted into the bedroom. "Hook the door." She felt a bit nervous giving Ted such explicit presents, but the idea excited her sufficiently that she managed to fetch the gifts despite her trembling hands.

Ted placed the hook into the bracket so the children wouldn't be able to enter unannounced. Lisa motioned him to the bed, and he sat on the edge. Then she put three carefully wrapped boxes in his lap and sat down beside him. She handed him the smallest one. "This one first."

Ted tore the Christmas wrap and stared at the box that was revealed. "Slick-um Lubricant," the printing exclaimed. "Slipperiest water-based gel available."

He pulled out the jar and held it up. "Neat idea," he said, his voice neutral.

"Just for fun," Lisa said.

"Okay," Ted said, opening the second package. "Deep-Stroking Dildo with Clitoral Stimulator," the second package said. "You're kidding," Ted said. "You got me a dildo?"

Lisa was suddenly not sure she had done the right thing. Maybe Ted would take the gifts as some negative comment on his lovemaking. "It's just a toy," she said, her voice now small and weak. "It's for us. I thought we could play sometime." Her voice trailed off.

"I think it's a great idea," Ted said, staring at his wife. "I just never thought you'd be interested in stuff like this." He reached over and quickly hugged her. "Fan-flippin'-tastic."

The grin that spread across his face was reward enough for Lisa. It had been very scary, but it was going to be worth it. She picked up the third package. "I don't know whether this will be your thing," she said, "but the idea turned me on." Then she giggled. "Remember that night a few weeks ago? I had just found this in the catalog."

"Oh," Ted said. "Oh!" He tore at the wrapping and saw a strange butterfly-shaped device. "Venus Butterfly," the box proclaimed. He read the explanation. "Did you get batteries?"

"They're included," Lisa said.

"Yeah." Ted fiddled with the heavy, two-inch in diameter, hot-pink plastic object and attached control box until he had the battery installed. "This is very interesting. Let's see just how it works," he said, a slightly professorial tone creeping into his voice. "Take your pants off." His leer belied his attempt to sound uninvolved.

Trembling with excitement and a bit of fear, Lisa removed her jeans and panties. As she started to unbutton her shirt, Ted took her hands. "For this to be a true test of how this thing works, I think we should have no additional stimulation. Lie down."

Lisa stretched out on the bed. The butterfly was attached to two elastic straps. "I think these go around your thighs," Ted said, slipping the loops around Lisa's feet and sliding them up her legs. He pulled the loops high on her hips so the butterfly pressed against her already wet pussy.

"Yipe, that's cold," Lisa said. Against her sizzling clit, it felt especially frigid.

"I'm really sorry about that," Ted said. He held a small plastic box that was connected to the butterfly with a slender wire. "Let's see whether this heats it up a bit." Lisa watched as Ted pushed a slide control with his thumb. "Oh God," she squealed as the item between her legs started to hum. "Oh shit, that's bad." She could feel the vibrations through her body, making her nipples suddenly erect and her back arch. "That's wicked," she puffed. "Oh God."

"Mmm," Ted purred, stretching out beside her, rubbing a finger over one erect nipple. "I like what this does to you." He played with the slider, speeding then slowing the vibrations. Then he leaned over and lightly bit the nipple that reached for his mouth.

The butterfly caused a deep hunger to blossom in Lisa's body. She wanted, needed to be filled. "Fuck me," she said.

"Not so fast," Ted said. "Just lie there and don't move. Let this baby do its worst."

"But I want you now," Lisa moaned.

"Not yet." Ted continued to play with the control, watching his wife's face flush and her head thrash back and forth. Sensing that she was getting close, he stood up and quickly removed his pants and shorts. In the still-rational part of his mind, he thought, it was very brave of Lisa to buy this stuff and suggest something new. Maybe I could, too. He lay back beside his wife, slowed the vibrations, then took her hand. He placed it against his hard cock and wrapped her fingers around it. "Stroke me," he said, his voice hoarse.

Lisa was only too happy to squeeze his cock and move her hand from the base to the tip. Suddenly she wanted to take him into her mouth, something she hadn't done in a long time. The device still quietly humming against her clit, she opened her eyes, slid downward on the bed, and looked at Ted. She held his cock near her face and smiled.

"Oh yes," he groaned. "Do it."

Lisa opened her mouth and took Ted's erection into its warm depths. She couldn't take it too deeply, but she flicked her tongue over the tip and sucked it hard. "Oh baby," Ted moaned. Unable to wait any longer, Ted pulled back, pulled the humming butterfly from Lisa's clit, and plunged into her sopping pussy.

Lisa reached between them and rubbed herself as Ted erupted deep inside her. She came only moments after her husband.

Later, still half-clothed, they lay side by side on the bed. "That was amazing," Ted said. "And we didn't even get to play with the other things."

"We'll get to those," Lisa said. "And there are several other items in the catalog I'd like to get."

"Maybe later we can both look through it." Ted winked. "Then we can see what develops."

# *Breasts*

I've never had perky breasts. Okay, I guess I've gotten used to it, but it's never made me happy. I guess I used to have some uplift, back before three pregnancies and lots of yo-yoing between my normal 34B and my pregnant 36D, so now—well, let's be honest—they droop. Now, however, I love it that they do. Let me tell you why.

One evening recently, we were watching an X-rated movie. We both enjoy a good erotic flick, although we have to wade through quite a few really awful ones to get to a decent one that turns us both on. That evening, we'd started to watch two really dreadful ones and turned them off halfway through. We thought we were doomed that evening, until we began one featuring a woman with large breasts. Well, I felt awful. Usually I can overlook the great silicone boobs on the porn stars, but that woman's face looked a bit like mine, and I couldn't help wishing my body looked as good as hers, silicone or no silicone.

I sighed, and Jack, my husband, wrapped an arm around my shoulder. "I know," he said. "Another loser."

We'd had a few beers, and I guess my tongue wasn't as tight as it should have been. "It's not that," I said. "I would love to have a body like hers."

"I love your body just the way it is."

Yeah, yeah, the usual reassurance. Actually, I think he really means it, but that evening it didn't help. I remained silent. Since this was the last of our rentals, we let the film play out. Somewhere down the line, the woman cradled her lover's cock between her more-than-ample breasts, and he did her that way, ending with a dramatic come shot. I felt Jack sigh. "Another boring come shot?" I asked.

"I guess," he said.

The way he said it made my radar extend to it fullest. Something was inside his brain. "What's up?" I said softly, hoping he'd share what was bothering him. He just motioned to the TV. What was going on? "Yes?" I whispered.

"I guess I've always wanted to do that."

"Come between a great set of breasts like that?" I said, feeling jealous.

"Come between any set of breasts."

"You've never said anything," I said, surprised. We'd been married almost four years, and I thought I knew just about everything regarding his sexual desires.

"I know. It just seems so kinky."

"And so impossible." I looked down at my small, droopy breasts.

"Does the idea turn you off?"

"Not at all. It's just . . ." I lifted my tee shirt to expose my bra. I unhooked the front clasp, and my breasts fell out.

Jack's breathing quickened. "You mean you'd let me?"

He wasn't getting it. "You mean you'd want to?"

That was all it took. He leaned down, and lifted one breast and licked the nipple. My nipples are very sensitive, and Jack knows it, so his playing and the beer made my pussy swell. I turned on the sofa, stifling my feelings of inadequacy. For several minutes Jack played with my breasts, kneading, fondling, sucking and licking, until I was really hot. I reached down and pressed my palm against the bulge in his jeans, and was surprised at how hard he was.

We quickly moved to the bedroom and removed all our clothing. His hands were everywhere—on my breasts, my thighs, between my legs, playing with my clit, stroking, rubbing. He inserted two fingers and fucked my pussy, coating his fingers with my juices, already flowing freely. Then he rubbed the wetness in the valley between my tits. He continued, making me wetter and wetter. He thrust his cock into my pussy, then rose and straddled my waist. He bent until his sopping cock was resting on my breastbone, then said, his voice gravelly, "Hold them. Please."

I lifted my breast flesh until his hardness was buried in the valley, then slid them up until the head of his cock poked out the top. I leaned over and flicked my tongue over the tip, the way the woman had done in the film. He pulled back, then thrust again, and again I licked.

As Jack continued to thrust between my breasts, I looked up at him. I'd seldom seen such a look of complete rapture on his face. "Shit, baby," he said, "I'm going to come."

I knew he would shoot on my face, and I sort of prepared myself. And indeed, he came with a roar, semen spurting, hitting my chin and dribbling down my neck. It was wonderful. I'd never seen Jack so excited and so satisfied. He collapsed on top of me, and we rolled over until we were side by side, both breathing hard.

We must have dozed, then Jack pulled the covers over us. "That was amazing," he said. "I know you didn't come. What can I do?"

Isn't he wonderful, I thought. "Nothing. Your orgasm was so wonderful, I don't need anything more."

"God, it was fabulous. I never thought you'd go for this. I

know you're self-conscious about your breasts, so I never asked."

"You should have. I hate that my tits droop, but that did help when it came to what we did."

"Yeah, it sure did. You're the best."

I guess I am.

# The Sculptor

He had been crafting the life-sized statue of the fertility goddess for over a month, barely sleeping or eating, trying to create a work worthy of Shanna herself. He had been honored when he heard that he'd received the job. He, a lowly carver who, until then, had crafted only small objects for the temple. Now he was to create the goddess herself.

First he had chosen the finest maple with just the right grain. Then he had stared at the piece of wood for several days, turning it, rubbing it lovingly with his palms, until the wood revealed the statue inside. Yes, he had thought, right there. There was the goddess, and he knew that he could set her free. And he did.

He fashioned the statue with sure strokes of his tools, until the magnificent naked woman appeared. He made her as he knew she would look if she were to come to life: her face open and accessible, her hair long and straight and hanging to her wide hips, her eyes gently gazing at those kneeling at her feet, her mouth sensual with soft lips. He made her body luscious yet not overblown—smooth breasts with large nipples, a slightly rounded belly, long, shapely legs. Her arms were spread, her hands open, as if welcoming supplicants and worshippers to her. He worked until she was at the same time magical, able to bring life to the land and its people, and a goddess for the people, easy to talk to, to ask for favors. She was the tribe's ideal. She was his ideal. Shanna, the goddess of all that is feminine and loving. Tomorrow he would present her to the priests of the temple, and they would install her in the place of honor, to live there forever. But for this last night, she was his.

He stroked the wooden body, adding the dampness from his hands to the fragrant oil he had rubbed on her body for many hours until he knew her body as well as he knew his own. He was resigned to the fact that he would take her to the temple the following morning, and he was glad that the people would finally have an image worthy of Shanna. Yet he was reluctant to part with her, his ideal woman. As the fire in his hut burned, he gazed at the beautiful statue, imagining.

In the darkest part of the night, when the fire in his hut was reduced to embers, he fell asleep. He didn't quite know what had awakened him, but he knew from the dim light that it was not yet dawn. He lay still, wondering what had aroused him. Had someone come into his hut? To steal the statue? He had a moment of panic, then he thought better of it. Of course they could not steal his goddess. The statue was far too big to steal. Then why was someone in his hut? He knew there was someone there; he could hear soft breathing, almost like a sigh. He could sense movement. Someone was definitely there in the darkness.

Slowly he turned onto his back and moved one arm. Something soft. He felt soft, warm flesh, the thigh of the one in the hut with him, obviously lying beside him on his furs. He should be afraid, he thought, but he realized that for some reason he wasn't. Who was here? He moved his hand slowly along the warm flesh. The skin was smooth as he ran his hand over it. He opened his eyes then and strained to see who was beside him, but it was too dark. He could make out only a shadow, a slightly thicker part of the darkness.

"Who is here?" he whispered.

"Don't you know me?"

The woman's voice was unfamiliar yet so loving. The tone was low, almost a purr, a melody that, once heard, couldn't be forgotten. "No, I don't, but I want to." He knew that he wanted to know this woman more than anyone he had ever met.

She laughed, a soft sound deep in her throat. "I want to know you too," she said. She took his hand and lifted it to her naked breast. "We should know each other at least once."

His hand filled with her flesh, the nipple erect against his palm. She was so warm, so soft, that he felt his body react despite his exhaustion. "Who are you?" he whispered.

"Shanna."

Had she said that, or had he merely dreamed it? Was that word real or just a sigh? As his fingers kneaded her full breast, he found he didn't care. He wanted, needed. And she was willing to give to him.

He lifted his other hand and placed it on her other breast. Now both his hands were filled, and he was in heaven. Her hands covered his, and she pressed his palms against her, soft sounds filling her throat. "Yes," she whispered. Again, a sigh or a word?

Her mouth found his, and the rapture was almost more than he could bear. His eyes closed, and his lips covered hers. Her tongue reached for his, and they stroked and dueled, growing more intimate each moment. Her hand cupped his head, threading her fingers through his hair, holding him so his mouth made more perfect contact with hers. The kiss seemed to last forever, yet it was over in an instant. As she pulled back, he felt a sense of overwhelming loss.

But then her hands were on his chest, stroking the lightly furred skin, fingers combing, exploring. As her hands roamed, so did his, gliding over her shoulders, her arms, her belly. Then her lips touched his again, and he was filled with images—mouths, breasts, engorged lower lips. And he suddenly hungered, a hunger greater than any he had ever had for a woman. His member hardened and lengthened. He wanted her more than he had ever wanted.

As they went on, her body pressed against his, the length of her against the length of him. She was heat and passion, and her hips strained against his. One hand splayed over his buttocks, pressing his hardness against her soft belly.

She moved back so that, with their lips still fused, her hand could find his erection. Her fingers wrapped around him and squeezed lightly. "Oh, yes," she breathed, and she stroked the length of him. "I want this."

He had never been so hot, so hungry, for any woman. His sex was larger, harder, as she moved her fingers, lightly pulling, then pushing. His hips moved so his member thrust into her hand, his precome making it slippery. Then she chuckled with the wonder of it all, the warmth of her joy filling him. "Oh, yes," she sighed.

She rolled onto her back, bringing him over on top of her. Lips still joined, she guided him into her wetness, and he found the most perfect home for his sex. It was as though he was meant to be there, part of her. He withdrew, then pressed in again, over and over, harder and harder, deeper and deeper. He pulled his mouth away, unable to breathe. Both her hands found his buttocks and pressed him still deeper into her. Her legs wrapped around his waist, holding him to her, as he roared and, too soon, his seed poured into her.

He must have slipped into unconsciousness then, and when he awoke, it was morning, sun streaming into his hut. What had happened? Who? Who? His eyes found the statue. Shanna. As he stared at her, he wondered. Could it have been? He gazed at her face. Had she always had that mysterious half-smile? Had he carved that expression?

He found he was deeply sad. He might never have that magical joining again. There could be no one as perfect for him. Yet he knew that what they had shared was for only one night and there would be another for him. Eventually.

"Manta, are you almost ready for the ceremony?" a female voice asked from just outside the hut. "We are waiting for you to let us in so we can move the beloved one to her temple."

That must be Lara, he thought, one of the servants of the goddess, the one who had brought him food he didn't eat during his frenzy of carving. He smiled. Yes, there would be others for him. He gazed at Shanna, his small smile matching hers. "Thank you," he whispered, "for showing me how it can be. How it will be."

He jumped. Had she nodded at him? No, it couldn't be. Could it?

# Cast

Have you ever been in a full leg cast? I would guess not. But I have. I am. Let me tell you that it hurts, it itches, it sucks. I don't even deserve it, really. This idiot driver pulled out in front of me, with no warning, no signal, no nothing. Needless to say, I totaled my Harley. In the hospital they told me I was very lucky that I didn't total myself. My helmet saved my brain, and my leather saved most of my skin. However, my leg was messed up pretty bad.

So here I am, in a cast from heel to crotch, stretched out on my bed with the TV remote for company, dressed in the only pair of boxers that fit over the damn plaster. My girlfriend stops by every day before and after work. Anne. She's the best thing to have happened to me in a long time. Not much to look at, but she's really been a lifesaver through this thing, and I've really found out that looks don't matter when it comes to a long-term relationship.

Before this, we had gone out for a month. Good times, and we'd had sex twice. Not bad. Not great, but not bad. Now sex is out. It's not that the doctor said I can't; it's just that I can't. Not with this monstrosity on my leg.

Anne has kept me sane. She plays card games with me; watches sports, which I know she doesn't really like; gets me all three meals, beers, everything I could want. In return, I bitch at her, complain and am generally a pain in the ass. I guess that if we can survive this, we can survive anything. Maybe this will actually turn into something long-term.

I was dozing one evening when Anne showed up just before six, with a pizza and a six-pack. Pepperoni and mushroom, just the way I like it. So we ate, drank and talked. "I brought something I thought you would like," she said, pulling a small plastic bag from her tremendous purse. Inside was a bottle of body lotion. "I thought you'd like a back rub, to get some of the kinks out."

My first thought was no. Rubbing some sweet-smelling, flowery goo over me wasn't my idea of fun and games. On second thought, however, my back was stiff, and a back rub might just feel good.

So we took a few minutes to get me rearranged. It's not an easy task to turn over these days. Anyway, soon I was flat and Anne was pouring lotion on her hands. "I warmed it in the microwave," she said, "so it should be a good temperature."

The first touch of her hands on me was heaven. Did I tell you she's a physical therapist? Now I know why her patients love her. She's got great hands. She kneaded the muscles of my back, and I found myself relaxing. Unfortunately, the relaxation of my back was leading to a lack of relaxation on my front. I was getting hard, and it was embarrassing. Here she was being kind and helpful, and I was thinking lecherous thoughts about her hands on my body. Stop it! I told myself.

She took a moment and put some music on the stereo. Something New Agey and very sexy. Sexy? Was that music sexy, or were her hands controlling my mind? She added more lotion and pulled the back of my shorts down so she could massage my buttocks. God, my cock was getting uncomfortable. I moved a bit to ease its cramped position, hoping she wouldn't notice.

When her thumbs separated my cheeks and rubbed the skin that hands rarely touch, I thought I'd erupt right then. Okay. Think about other things. I counted the dots on the sheet under my face, did the times tables, calculated batting averages, and all the time, her hands were supposedly soothing my skin.

"That's wonderful," I said, "but your hands must be getting tired. You can stop now."

"Oh, no," she said. "I was just about to have you turn over so I could do your front."

Do your front? I knew exactly which part of my front needed doing. But Anne's a nice, conservative girl, I thought. If I turn over, she'll see my hard-on and run screaming. She's not ready for this.

"Come on, I'll help you turn over." She moved the sheet beneath me and sort of flipped me over. Shit, I thought. The end of a wonderful relationship.

Well, she didn't bat an eye, but poured lotion in her hands and began to rub my chest. It took only moments for me to discover that I have very sensitive nipples. Every time her fingers slid over them, my cock jerked. They puckered like Anne's do when she's aroused. I pressed my eyes closed and thought about cold showers. Slowly she worked on my pecs, then moved down to my abs. "I love your body," she said. "I work on a lot of men, but you've got the best chest I think I've ever seen."

"Thanks," I said, blessing my hours in the gym.

I thought that she accidentally brushed my cock, until she said, "It seems you have a bit of a problem here."

My eyes flew open. She was grinning, licking her lips. "I checked with your doctor, and he says there's no reason not to do it."

"Do what?" I choked out.

She said nothing, just pulled down my shorts and grabbed my cock. "This," she said, slowly rubbing her slippery hands over my hard-on. "Baby," I said, "this is wonderful, but . . ."

"But what?" she said. "Let me."

Let her? She had one hand around the base of my cock and the other cupping my balls, squeezing lightly. I would have begged. "Let me," she whispered, her mouth slowly lowering.

"Baby," I groaned. "Oh, God, baby."

She rubbed, stroked, then her tongue flicked over the tip of my cock and lapped at the precome that oozed from it. I moaned. I couldn't help it. I was going to come right then.

"Not yet," she purred, and she didn't let me come. She gripped the base of my shaft hard, preventing the come that boiled in my testicles from erupting. It was exquisite torture. Obviously she wanted to be in charge, so I lay back and closed my eyes. I surrendered to the feelings, her hands, her tongue slowly licking the head, then the stalk, of my penis. She knew exactly where to touch.

I thought I couldn't get any higher, but I did. I couldn't move my hips with the cast, so I just had to lie still and let her masturbate me, and she did it like an expert. Suddenly she took my entire cock in her mouth and let go of the base. I came in a rush, filling her mouth with my come. I was so hot, I think I came for several minutes.

"What about you?" I asked when I was finally able to think again.

"Watch," she said, and she stood beside the bed, near my head. She was obviously wet, and I could smell the musky scent of her juices. She pulled off her slacks and panties, leaving her shirt on. Then she climbed onto the bed and sat cross-legged about a foot from my face. "Watch," she said, dipping her hand into the valley between her legs. I focused on her fingers as they slid through her glistening folds. She clips her pussy hair short, so I could see every movement. She made small cooing noises and moaned from time to time as she manipulated her clit. "Stick your fingers in," she said, her voice hoarse, her breathing rapid.

I obliged, filling her slippery channel with first one, then— as she yelled "More!"—two, then three. She continued to rub her clit, her gasps loud and coming faster and faster. "Yes," she cried, and I felt her pussy muscles clench in waves. I'd never felt anything like those squeezes on my fingers.

She collapsed beside me, and I think we slept.

I jerked awake when I heard the front door slam. "Hi, Greg," Anne's voice called. "I brought pizza—pepperoni and mushroom, just as you like it."

Had that incredible interlude been just a dream? I shook my head to clear it. Although I could smell the aroma of her pussy in my head, my nose sensed nothing. No lotion smell either. My chest and my skin felt normal, not slick with oil. Shit. I'd had a wet dream. I looked down and discovered that I hadn't really ejaculated. That was lucky, since I wasn't sure how Anne would react. The real one, not the one from my dream.

Shit. "Thanks, Anne. Pizza's great."

"I also brought some lotion. I thought a back rub might be nice."

Nice? Maybe . . .

# Cock Teaser

Eric had been dating Sue for almost two months, and he had been getting nowhere, fast. It isn't that Sue doesn't like me, Eric thought. We have lots of fun together and never seem to run out of things to talk about. And she tells me that I turn her on, but her body tells me that I don't.

Eric and Sue had never been to bed together. Their dates usually ended with fifteen or twenty minutes of necking at either Sue's house or Eric's apartment, which Sue would cut short with one of a variety of excuses. On their last date, Eric had decided to confront Sue when, after thirty minutes of necking, Sue had suddenly developed a headache. Eric's cock was hard and swollen, and his balls were aching. Although he was angry, he responded in his usual calm and considerate manner, not letting his anger show. "Sue, you know I like you a lot, but sex doesn't seem to be working out between us. Maybe we should just be friends."

"Oh, please, Eric," Sue said. "I want to be more than friends with you. I just need a little more time. You're so considerate. I know you'll give me a chance to show you how much you turn me on the next time we get together."

Eric gave in, as he always did, and went home with his balls swollen and aching.

The movie had been great, and they had been talking about it all the way home. As they pulled into the driveway of Sue's house, Sue smiled at Eric and asked, "Would you like to come in for a while?"

"Oh, I don't know, Sue," Eric said. "That movie was pretty erotic, and frankly, I'm horny as hell. I'm not sure I can be trusted."

"I trust you," Sue replied teasingly. "I know you wouldn't rape me, would you?"

"Of course not," Eric answered. "But I'm not sure I want to get all turned on and end up going home frustrated again."

"It'll be different tonight. I promise," Sue replied.

They entered the house, and Sue said, "Why don't you sit down on the sofa, and I'll fix us some drinks." As Eric relaxed on the sofa, he could hear the tinkle of ice cubes as Sue prepared Bloody Marys for each of them. Sue brought the drinks in, then sat beside him. As Eric sipped his drink, he could feel the cold and the heat of the drink slide down his throat, both cooling and warming his insides, down to his balls. He looked at Sue's large breasts pressing against the rather prim blouse that she was wearing, as if eager to break free of their restraints, then looked up at her pretty face. She had seen his gaze and had leaned back a little to make her nipples press harder against her blouse.

Eric felt his cock harden inside his pants as he looked at Sue. He put his drink down, then reached over and took Sue's drink out of her hand and put it on the table. He put his arm around her, drew her close and gently brushed his lips against hers. She responded by pressing her lips against his and opening her mouth so that he could explore her mouth with his tongue. As he slid his tongue between her lips and penetrated her mouth, he gently stroked her nipples through her blouse. He could feel them harden and tighten as he stroked, and Sue pressed her breast against his hand, as if she wanted more. As Eric caressed Sue's tongue with his own, he gently caressed the inside of her thigh. The softness and warmth of her flesh made his cock even harder, and his balls began to ache. Eric began to fuck Sue's mouth with his tongue as his fingers slid between her legs and stroked her mound through her now-wet panties. She moaned as he slid his fingers along the inside edge of her panties, stroking the crease, then sliding under and gently stroking her wet slit.

"Oh, baby," Sue moaned, "you're so gentle."

Eric prided himself on his considerate lovemaking, and continued to stroke Sue gently even though she pressed her cunt against his hand as if asking for something more.

After twenty minutes of gently touching and stroking Sue's breasts and nipples and sliding his fingers along her slit, pausing to stroke her clit, Eric felt like he was about to burst. But he couldn't help noticing that Sue's breathing had slowed down. Her nipples were no longer hard, and her cunt was not as wet as before. "Let's go into the bedroom," he suggested.

"Oh, I forgot, Eric," she replied. "I have an early appointment at the hairdresser tomorrow morning." I really need to get to bed early. I'm really sorry. I hope you don't mind. Maybe next time." Sue looked at him sheepishly, a small smile on her face, waiting for his response.

Eric was literally squirming to ease the pressure on his cock. He wanted to unzip his fly, release his cock and say to Sue, "Suck my cock, you bitch, and don't stop until I've spurted into your throat and you've swallowed every drop." As he looked at the little smile on Sue's face, he thought she was actually enjoying watching him squirm. She's getting off on it, he thought. He felt his rage boil up until it replaced the ache in his balls. He had been about to say, "It's all right, baby. I don't mind," but instead found his anger erupting like a powerful ejaculation.

"Fuck you, bitch!" he roared. "You can suck my dick, you slut!" Eric stood up. "I'm going home and jerking myself off, or maybe I'll just pick up a hooker on the street. At least she'll be honest and give what she promises. I don't ever want to have anything to do with you again."

As Eric strode toward the door, Sue tried to grab his arm. He shook her off, violently, and continued toward the door. Sue ran after him and grabbed his upper arm in a viselike grip.

"Please don't go, Eric," she pleaded.

Eric tried to shake her off again, but she clung to him with all her strength.

"Please, Eric, give me another chance."

He turned and faced her.

"Why the fuck should I, bitch? You're just a fucking cock teaser."

"You don't understand, Eric. Just give me a chance to make you understand."

"What don't I understand, slut?"

"I can't explain in words," Sue replied. "Just let me make it up to you. I know I've treated you badly."

As they faced each other, Sue lowered her eyes and stared at the floor. "I've been very bad, and I should be punished," she said softly.

Still angry, Eric continued to shout. "Fuck that, bitch! I just want to get the fuck out of here!"

Standing in front of Eric, with her head still lowered, Sue said something so softly that Eric could not understand what she had said.

"What's that, slut? I can't hear a word you're saying!" he shouted.

They stood facing each other silently, Eric glaring and Sue with her head lowered. "If you stay, you can punish me for my bad behavior. You can spank me, as hard and as long as you want," she said, almost in a whisper.

As Eric stared at Sue, standing submissively in front of him, his anger disappeared and was replaced by confusion. He had never been anything but kind, gentle and considerate with women. As he looked at Sue, he saw that her nipples were again pressing hard against her blouse, and her breasts were rapidly rising and falling. As she timidly raised her eyes to meet his, he could see that they were bright and gleaming, and the pupils of her lovely brown eyes were widely dilated. He knew, instinctively, that if he were to place his hand between her legs, he would find her sopping wet. He realized that excitement had now replaced his anger, that he was being given an opportunity to do something different, to explore another part of himself, and that he might never have such an opportunity again. He made his decision.

"You have been a very bad girl, Suzie," he said quietly but in a no-nonsense manner, gazing into her eyes. They seemed to brighten even more as he spoke. "I think that a severe spanking is the appropriate punishment for such a bad girl."

Sue lowered her eyes. "Are you going to spank me very hard?" she asked, her voice trembling.

"You will look at me when you speak to me, Suzie," Eric ordered. "And you will address me as sir."

Sue raised her head and gazed into Eric's eyes. He thought that he had never seen her look so beautiful.

"Will it hurt a lot?" she asked.

"Oh, yes, Suzie. You know that you've been bad, don't you?"

"Yes, sir."

"Well, then, the spanking will have to be appropriately hard. Won't it, Suzie?"

Sue lowered her eyes. Eric knew that she was embarrassed for him to see the excitement in her eyes.

"Look at me when I speak to you, Suzie!" Eric barked.

Sue's head snapped up. "Yes, sir. But please don't hurt me too much."

"It will be as much as I feel is necessary," Eric replied. "Your pleas or cries will have no influence on me."

"Can I keep my panties on?"

"Oh, no," Eric chuckled. "That wouldn't be appropriate at all. No, Suzie, I am going to sit on the sofa, and you are going to lie across my lap. Then I will raise your skirt and bunch it up around your waist. Then I will pull your panties down around your ankles, and you will wait that way, with your pretty ass naked and exposed, until I decide to begin your spanking." As Eric spoke, he saw that Sue's breathing rate had increased even more, and her face was flushed with excitement.

"Are you going to use your hand?" Sue asked, her voice catching in her throat.

"No, Suzie. I noticed a ruler on the desk in your study. Go and fetch it for me. And then go into the bathroom and get a bottle of baby oil. Your ass is going to need something to soothe it by the time I'm finished."

Sue slowly walked out of the room and returned with a fifteen-inch plastic ruler and a small bottle of baby oil. She handed both to Eric. He could see that her hand was trembling. Eric examined the ruler, flexed it, then slapped it against the palm of his hand as Sue watched. "Yes, I think this will do fine," he said. He strode over to the sofa and sat down. "Get over here, Suzie," he ordered. "Enough talking. It's time for your spanking."

Sue walked over to Eric and stood in front of him. "Well," he said, "you know what to do now."

Silently, Sue lay facedown across Eric's lap and buried her face in a pillow. Without another word, Eric raised her skirt to her waist and, in one swift motion, pulled her panties down to her ankles. Eric let her lie with her naked ass in the air so that she could anticipate the spanking while he thought about what he was about to do. It occurred to him that no one had ever trusted him as much as Sue was trusting him now. She had set no limits for what he now realized was an incredibly exciting sexual exploration for both of them. She trusted that he would not hurt her so much that it would spoil the pleasure for both of them. But he knew that she was also trusting him to be firm enough. If he were too gentle, that would also spoil it. He determined that he would be true to his role.

Eric took the ruler and began slapping it hard against the palm of his hand. He could see Sue's buttocks begin to quiver. "Are you ready for your spanking, Suzie?" he asked.

"I'm afraid," Suzie said. "It's going to hurt."

"Of course it will," Eric replied. "And you can cry as much as you want to. But if you try to get away and I have to hold you down, your punishment will be twice as much. Do you understand?"

"Yes, sir," Sue answered.

Eric gently stroked Sue's trembling ass. "Your beautiful little ass feels so cool now. But I'm going to make it very hot. Are you ready?"

Sue's "Yes, sir" was muffled by the pillow.

Eric raised the ruler and brought it down hard on the center of Sue's ass, leaving a horizontal red streak across both cheeks. Sue's cry was muffled by the pillow. Eric continued to rhythmically spank Sue with the ruler, until her entire ass was a bright pink color. He couldn't tell if her muffled cries were of pain or pleasure, or both, but she was meekly accepting her punishment. At last he decided that the spanking was enough. "You have been very cooperative, Suzie," he said. "You've taken your spanking like a good girl. I'm proud of you."

"Can I get up now, sir?" Sue whimpered.

"No, Suzie. Not yet. I'm going to put some baby oil on your pretty red ass to cool the burning. Just lie still." Eric squeezed the plastic bottle and coated his fingers with the oil. Then he gently began applying it to the inflamed skin of Sue's buttocks. "Does that feel better, Suzie?" he asked.

Sue sniffled, "Oh, yes, sir. Thank you, sir."

Eric let his fingers slide between Sue's legs and felt that she was sopping wet. She gasped as he stroked her clitoris, then cried out as, without any preamble, he plunged two fingers deep into her cunt. Her hips bucked as he finger-fucked her as she lay across his lap with her hot cheeks, now shiny with oil, in the air.

Eric withdrew his fingers from Sue's cunt. "Get up. I want you completely naked. Right now," Eric said. Sue wriggled off Eric's lap, stood up and began to remove her clothes. By the time Eric had ripped off his pants, shirt and underpants, she was standing in front of him naked. Eric roughly pushed her back onto the sofa, kneeled over her, spread her legs apart and, without another word, drove his swollen cock into her dripping cunt. Although she had only whimpered during her spanking, Sue now shrieked with pleasure as Eric pinched her nipples hard while slamming his engorged penis into her body. She came again and again, and as Sue was rocked by orgasm after orgasm, Eric exploded into her cunt.

\*    \*    \*

They lay naked, holding each other, on the narrow sofa. Both were drained. "Now do you understand?" Sue asked.

"Yes, Sue, I understand completely. And from now on, when you forget what happens to bad girls, I'll have to pull your panties down and remind you."

Sue raised an eyebrow. "You know, Eric," she said. "Boys sometimes forget their manners and need to be punished too."

# Fellatio

"You know I want to please you," Marla said to her husband of two years, Jeff. "I just can't do it. It's not that I don't want to give you oral sex. I do. It's just that my throat closes up and I just can't." A tear trickled down Marla's face.

Jeff was really distraught. He had never said that he wanted it, although he did. His fantasies all revolved around his lovely wife's mouth surrounding his cock. Just the thought of her lips on him made him hard, but he'd never asked for it. Ever. He knew how she felt. Her ex-husband had held the back of her head and forced her to fellate him, and now it had become such an issue that he'd do anything to make the whole thing go away. "Baby, you don't have to. I'd never ask you to do anything you didn't want to."

Sniffling, Marla said, "I know that. But I want to so much. I know the thought excites you, and I want to give this to you." She used a tissue, then said, "I got an idea from an article in a magazine. If you'll let me do whatever I want, it just might work."

"If it will give you pleasure, I'll let you do anything you want. You know that."

Marla's watery grin was reward enough. And if she'd actually do it, well . . .

The following evening, they had dinner at a neighborhood Italian restaurant—spaghetti with clam sauce and several beers. Just to loosen me up, Marla thought. She'd planned everything, but she still wasn't sure she could go through with it. Jeff was such a wonderful man, and she knew how much he wanted this. She also knew that she was being silly about oral sex.

In the beginning, with her ex-husband, Tom, she'd enjoyed it, both for its own sake and for the joy it gave him. However, eventually it had become a battle. It was never her choice, only his. When he wanted her to suck him, he'd demand and she'd comply. Eventually, he began to just ram his big cock down her throat when he was in the mood. He'd straddle her chest, fists in her hair, and unable to move, she'd part her lips, and he'd fuck her mouth until his semen poured down her throat. He'd done that twice before she'd walked out.

Now he was history. She and Jeff had met almost a year after her divorce was final, and their sex life had always been wonderful, a loving sharing of pleasures. Now she wanted to perform oral sex on him, but her experiences tainted the joy.

But she had a plan.

They walked home from the restaurant, both a little tipsy, giggling about the least little thing. As Jeff fumbled for his key, Marla asked, "Are you ready for anything?"

"Anything?"

"Anything."

"Okay, I'm game." He opened the front door, and they walked into the darkened house. "What's next?"

"Go into the bedroom and get naked. Then lie down on the bed, and I'll be in shortly."

Marla watched Jeff's back as he walked down the short hallway. When he was out of sight, she quickly stripped until she was down to her bra and panties, new ones she'd bought at Victoria's Secret just for this evening. She picked up a plastic bag of stuff for the games to come and followed Jeff's path through the apartment.

As she entered the bedroom, Jeff was lying on the wide bed, naked, his cock semi-erect, a small smile on his face. "Wow! That outfit is sexy as hell."

Reflexively she looked down at the tiny bits of black lace that covered her breasts and mound. From the widening of Jeff's pupils, she knew she'd chosen well. "Glad you like it," she said, her voice low and throaty. "I'm Candy, and I'm so glad you bought me for the evening to give you pleasure. Are you ready for me?"

"I'm ready for whatever you have in mind," he said. "Seriously, Marla, you know you never have to do anything, just be your own sexy self."

"I'm not my sexy self. I'm Candy." She'd reasoned that becoming someone else might help her to get past her reluctance. "I'm going to tie you up now."

"You're going to what?"

Marla raised an eyebrow. "You heard me," she said, taking a length of soft cotton clothesline from the bag. "Give me your wrist."

Jeff held out his left arm, and Marla looped the end of the long rope around his wrist, then around the corner of the headboard of the bed. She threaded the rope around the back of the headboard, then tied his other wrist. "So you can't do anything." Including hold my head.

With little fuss, she eventually tied both his ankles to the legs of the bed. Finally she stepped back and gazed at her handiwork. "Nice," she purred. "All mine." She giggled. "Now don't run away."

Jeff's grunt was all she wanted to hear.

Jeff had never been tied up before, and he found it mildly arousing, but that wasn't the point. He knew that Marla was planning to try oral sex and, after her ex-husband's oral rape of her, the idea that his hands were tied must make her feel safer. Good idea. He heard water running in the bathroom, then Marla returned with a basin filled with water, scented with his aftershave. "I want to make you smell like you," she said, "all sexy and spicy."

Slowly she washed his hands and arms, then ran the soft cloth over his chest. His legs were next. He found the process slightly erotic, and he felt his cock begin to stir. When she arrived at his inner thighs and then washed his balls, he knew he was getting harder. Finally she began to stroke his erection with the cloth, ever so slowly rubbing the length of him. She'd always been good at hand jobs, and she was obviously using every trick she knew to get him hard. It was working. Very well.

"Mmm," she purred. "Such a lovely cock you have." She put the basin and cloth on the floor, then pulled something from her plastic bag. "This is Hershey's Syrup, and this is whipped cream," she said. "I'm going to create a penis sundae." She took a large plastic sheet from the bag and had Jeff lift his butt so she could shove it beneath him. "Next time I'll remember to do this first."

"Whatever," he mumbled as he watched her hands slowly open the bottle of chocolate.

"This will make you taste *sooo* delicious," she said. "I'll just want to lick and lick and lick."

With each repetition of the word 'lick' his cock got harder.

As Marla watched Jeff's cock grow, she knew this would work, and she grinned. Not only was she going to get past her reluctance, she was going to give Jeff the time of his life. Slowly she drizzled the chocolate sauce over his erection. As the thin, dark brown stream landed on his skin, his cock twitched. She put the syrup down, bent over and licked the length of him, marveling at both the taste and the feel of his cock.

"Oh, God, baby, that's torture."

She giggled. "Yes. It is. Candy loves chocolate." Candy. The person who could do all the things Marla couldn't. "And whipped cream." She shook the can, then squirted white foam all over Jeff's crotch. "It might take me quite a while to lick all this off."

And lick she did, all over his crotch area, and from his moans, she knew Jeff was really hot. When she'd first read the article, she'd laughed at the idea of chocolate and whipped cream, but now she realized that it was just what she needed.

Eventually, when all the whipped cream was gone, Marla poured more chocolate on his rock-hard cock. She looked in his eyes, needing to be serious for just a moment. "I need you to keep yourself from coming in my mouth," she said. "Just for now. Eventually . . ."

"It's fine," Jeff said.

"When you need to come, just tell me."

"God, I need to come right now," he moaned, "but this is too good to ask you to stop."

"I trust you," she said, and she realized that she did. She licked the length of his erection, then took the head between her lips. He couldn't hold her, she knew, with his hands tied, so she could dictate the depth and speed of her sucks. Slowly she drew him more deeply into her mouth, then created a slight vacuum and pulled back. Deeper, then back, she fucked her mouth with his cock for several moments, until he yelled that he was going to come.

She sat back and wrapped her fingers around his penis as spurts of semen landed all over his belly. Leaving him tied up, she sat beside him, grinning. "God, baby," he panted, "I might never be able to come again."

"It was good?"

"Baby," he laughed, "it was orgasmic!" As she watched him with so much joy, he caught his breath. "But what about you? You didn't come."

"That's okay. Eventually I'll untie you." She looked at the chocolate sauce and whipped cream on the bed table. "There's quite a bit of stuff left over."

# The Hammock

**M**y husband has the most fertile imagination and is a whiz with tools. So every now and then, he comes up with a delicious new toy for us to play with. Let me tell you about his latest.

We live in a rather deserted area, and our next-door neighbors are almost a mile away. That amount of privacy permits us to do things out-of-doors that others might not be able to do. One more thing. I love hammocks. We have several of varying construction hanging between trees here and there. My favorite is one of the ones that has a wooden dowel across the top and the bottom, which Rob fastened loosely to two heavy branches so it can swing in any direction, not just side to side.

Well, that's the basis of Rob's latest toy. Let me see whether I can describe it for you. While I was away one day, he lengthened the dowel at the feet, and cut a V-shaped opening, wide at the dowel end and narrowing to a point right at the middle of the canvas, where my behind would be. Then he stretched the canvas to the ends of the dowel and tacked it there. Got the picture? The minute I saw it, I did.

With a delightful leer, Rob stripped me, lay me on the

contraption and used wide, soft pieces of fabric to tie my legs to the canvas. Thus my legs were spread as wide as they could be without being uncomfortable. He pulled my hands together beneath the seat of the swing and tied them securely with a length of soft rope. I was deliciously naked, in a dappling of sun and shade, unable to move. "Now just take," he said. "I won't brook any interference, so remain totally silent."

I love it when he just takes over completely, so I nodded. He would have this encounter his way. "Good girl," he said.

He pushed the swing so the breeze blew between my legs. I had never felt cool air blowing across my flesh like that. "I've got a few things to do inside," Rob said, and he disappeared into the house, leaving me alone with my erotic thoughts. Slowly I cooled down and just relaxed, enjoying the play of light and shadow, heat and coolness, over my exposed skin.

Finally, as I dozed, Rob returned, trailing a long extension cord. "I thought you might want this," he said, slowly inserting a vibrator into my now-calm pussy. Not calm for long. It took only a second for my juices to flow and my nipples to tighten. "And I brought these too," he said, dangling from his index finger a pair of nipple clamps with a long chain between them.

I knew what was going to happen, but I was unable to stop the erection of my nipples as he stroked my pussy with the vibrator. "Good," he said as he pinched one tight bud between his thumb and forefinger, then pulled it and fastened the clamp to my engorged flesh. He had modified it so that it was very tight when my nipples were erect but pinched just slightly when I was calm. Right then, it was just on the good side of painful.

He ran the chain beneath the hammock and up the other side, and clipped the second clamp to my other nipple.

Now, if I moved, the chain tightened and pulled at my tender flesh. It was the most delicious torture. Leaving the vibrator in my pussy, he went back into the house.

I know he was watching me from inside, but I didn't care. Slowly I became accustomed to the sensations, and my body calmed again. I was amazed that I could do that with a vibrator buzzing in my cunt, but I did. Suddenly the buzzing stopped and the dildo began some kind of in-and-out motion. My arousal rocketed to the top of the scale. Several minutes later, the movement stopped and the buzzing began again. Somehow, as he watched, Rob could tell when I was calming and could change the rhythm of the dildo to keep me at the edge of orgasm. With my hands and legs unable to move, I couldn't help myself over the edge. Several times I thought I could hear him chuckle.

He continued like that for more than half an hour, maintaining my arousal at its peak, then appeared beside me. "Ready?" he said, laughing.

"I've never been so ready in my life," I answered.

He removed the nipple clamps, and the flow of blood returning to my tits caused a fresh rush of heat through my body. How anyone could get higher than I was already I'll never know, but . . .

Rob pulled off his shorts, ducked beneath the hammock and stood between my legs. The canvas was at just the right height so his engorged cock was level with my pussy. God, he was hard. He stood there playing with the vibrator in my cunt with one hand and rubbing his erection with the other. I wanted him to touch my clit so I could come, but I knew he wouldn't make it that easy for me.

Finally, when his cock was as hard as it could get, he pulled the vibrator out and plunged his cock into me. God, it was heaven. The hammock/swing moved as he fucked me so I couldn't get a really tight hold. I squeezed my vaginal muscles to try to grip him in, but as the hammock moved, he pulled out, then pushed.

"God, baby," he cried, "this feels even better than I had imagined."

I thought he would let me come then, but suddenly he pulled out and settled on a short stool he had brought with him, his mouth against my pussy. His tongue is magic, and after only a moment of his mouth on my clit, I came. Hard. Long. Spasms rocked my body as I kept coming. He stood and rammed his cock home, and I continued screaming as I came again and again. As he always does, he bellowed as he came, the most wonderful sound I can imagine.

We've used that hammock often since then. Maybe next time I'll tell you about the afternoon I put him in it. Did you know that a man's nipples can be as sensitive as a woman's?

# For the Love of Diamonds

The darkness of the room could barely be penetrated by the tiny penlight he held in his hand. He shined the light from side to side, its tiny beam revealing the corners of the room, finally coming to rest on the woman who lay sleeping in the middle of a king-size bed, the covers gently rising and falling with her breathing.

God, she's beautiful, he thought to himself, as his eyes devoured her sleeping form. The porcelain white skin, which he knew was soft and silky to the touch, glowed in the light.

The front of his trousers bulged as he thought of the way she felt when he was inside her. There was no better feeling in the world than the sensation of silky hot pussy. He craved it almost above all else. Almost.

But the one thing he craved more, the reason he was here tonight, dressed in black from head to toe, his breath hot behind a black balaclava mask, was the icy glitter of diamonds!

Not the cheap, run-of-the-mill diamonds found at chain jewelry stores, but the blues and pinks and yellows with flawless cuts, in weights of four, five, six carats and more!

The kind you could see in stores only by appointment and buy with a black American Express card.

Dark curls spread out across the pillow as she slept. The corners of her mouth curved slightly from a dream-induced smile.

The intruder stole one last lingering look at the sleeping woman, before stealthily moving toward a large walk-in closet, where he knew she kept her safe.

Look at that! The safe was already open. What a trusting fool she is. She deserves to have her diamonds stolen!

The small light played across gold rings and sets of earrings lined up in velvet holders. Trays full of stuff he couldn't care less about.

His eyes lit up when he saw, there, way in the back, the object of his desire, the prize for which he was risking it all. Three princess-cut pink diamonds, each a full two carats, set in a platinum ring. From experience, he knew this one ring had an appraisal value of at least one hundred and ten thousand dollars. Probably closer to one hundred and fifty.

Just as his fingers closed on the ring, the lights flicked on. His whole body went still when he heard the voice behind him.

"Don't even fucking breathe, asshole!" Kaitlin's all-too-familiar voice said from the doorway to the closet he was trapped in. "I'm pointing a thirty-eight right at the back of your head!"

Ray could hear the footsteps muffled by the carpet as Kaitlin crept closer to him. His mind raced as he tried to come up with a way out of this mess. He felt the barrel of the gun press into his spine, as Kaitlin's other hand grasped and pulled the balaclava mask off.

"I knew you'd show up, Ray," Kaitlin's voice said huskily from behind him, her hot breath caressing his neck.

"You must've thought I was some kind of fool . . . that I

wouldn't notice how your eyes lit up every time I wore my ring."

"That's what you came for, right Ray? The ring? So go ahead, take it out."

Ray dared not move.

"I said, take it out, Ray!" Kaitlin insisted, the gun pressing harder into his back. Ray took the ring from the safe, an involuntary shudder coursing through his body as he held it in his hand.

"God, if I didn't know any better, I'd say you just had an orgasm!" Kaitlin said, a hint of humor in her voice, giving Ray momentary hope.

"Kaitlin, I can expl—"

"Can you, Ray? What could you possibly say that would justify your breaking into my house? Did you think because you have a nice, thick prick, and could fuck me to orgasm over and over again, making me come like no one ever has before, that you were entitled to take anything else you wanted?"

Ray wisely kept quiet, still hoping for a way out.

"You bastard!" Kaitlin murmured, her voice catching in her throat. "Take it Ray. Pull your dick out of your pants. I want to see it," she added, as her free hand caressed her pussy, her fingers sliding in between the silky folds, making herself wet.

Son of a bitch! I just might get out of this after all, Ray thought wildly as he unzipped his pants, his hard dick springing free.

"Jack it off, Ray. I want to see you jack yourself off."

"Kaitlin, can you at least take the gun off my back first? I can't concentrate with a thirty-eight so close to my spine."

"What? This thing?" Kaitlin said, laughing. "It's not even real!"

She tossed the gun on the floor, and when Ray turned around in surprise, he found Kaitlin completely naked.

Looking into her eyes, he took one of her hands and guided it to his throbbing dick. Her fingers closed around his shaft, and she bit her bottom lip, as desire flooded her body with warmth.

"Ahhh, God, Ray—lick my pussy, darling," Kaitlin moaned. "Please, baby. Lick me!"

Ray leaned into her and began to kiss her neck as Kaitlin's fingers entwined in his hair. Her head fell back in ecstasy as Ray trailed kisses down her stomach, until he was kneeling before her.

Kaitlin spread her legs in invitation, and Ray buried his face into her hot pussy, his tongue licking and lapping her sweet nectar, as he slid two fingers into her, finger-fucking her as he hungrily swallowed her wetness.

"Oh, my God, Ray! What are you doing to me? I'm gonna come! Oh, oh, put it in me, darling! I want to feel your beautiful dick inside me!"

Ray gave one last lick before lying back, pulling Kaitlin down on top of him. His swollen shaft was pressing against her soft opening, and Kaitlin slowly lowered herself onto him.

High-pitched moans escaped her parted mouth, and her hands came up to the sides of her head, her fingers running through the soft curls of her hair as she rocked back and forth on Ray's thick rod. "Oh, oh, oh, I'm coming, Ray. Oh, my God, yes! Yes! Yes!" she cried out as wave after wave of pleasure enveloped her body.

Ray arched his body upward, pushing deeper into Kaitlin's silky heat, as he exploded in orgasm, his hot come filling Kaitlin's pussy.

She collapsed on top of him, nestling her head into his shoulder, as she tried to catch her breath.

"Ray," she whispered after a few minutes had passed, their bodies still connected.

"Yeah?"

"You can have it."

"What?"

"The ring, Ray. You can have it."

"I can?" Ray asked in amazement. "You really mean it?"

"Sure," Kaitlin said as she snuggled closer to him. "It's a goddamn fake anyway!"

After a moment of stunned silence, Ray burst out laughing. He may have missed out on the diamonds, he thought to himself, but he was still holding one hell of a gem!

# Rob

I'd had him made to my exacting specifications by Robotics, Inc. All I'd wanted was a servant, someone (is that the right word for a cybernetic being?) to do chores, keep the house, cook meals, all the things that neither my wife nor I had time to do. That way, Marie and I would finally have some time to do the things she and I wanted to do. Without all the time-consuming tasks that the servant would be doing, we could go to movies, sit with our feet up and watch TV, go bowling or play cards with friends. It would be fabulous.

Robotics, Inc., was all too willing to please, for a fee, of course. Rob—that's what Marie and I learned to call him—was given all the bells and whistles Robotics, Inc., had to offer: super-lifelike skin, regulated body temperature, real hair, the works. I knew that Marie wouldn't necessarily take to him immediately, so I selected the most pleasing male form I could find. (I'd first thought of a cute little maid type with extra long legs and big . . . Well, jealousy wouldn't do, so I'd ordered Rob.)

It took Marie no time at all to adjust. Rob was quiet, unobtrusive and remarkably efficient. Everything in the house was taken care of without any specific directions. He just pleased us by keeping the place in tip-top running order, and pleasing us is a robot's prime directive.

One afternoon, I arrived home unexpectedly early. My three o'clock meeting had been cancelled, and so I just split for the first time in months. I was looking forward to watching a tape of Super Bowl CII with a big bowl of chips and some of the onion-garlic dip Rob made so well. I knew that Marie often ended her workday at three, but I hoped this wasn't one of those days. I wanted time just for myself.

As I closed the front door behind me, I heard noises upstairs in our bedroom. Somehow the words "Pleasing Us" echoed through my mind. No. It couldn't be. With all his human-looking skin and gorgeous male physique, he wasn't anatomically correct, so what I was hearing wasn't an option, was it? Curious, I tiptoed up the stairs and down the hall to our bedroom. The noises weren't difficult to identify. Marie's grunts and squeals were unmistakable.

It's funny, but I didn't feel jealous. We lived in a pretty free society, after all. What I did feel was just plain curious. I was dying to know what they were doing. The second bedroom shared a wraparound porch with ours, so I thought I'd just slip out and peep in through the sliding-glass doors. I knew that when I opened the glass door to get to the porch, the noise would be obvious, however. And anyway, the sounds were abating. Everything must be over. I scurried silently back down the stairs, opened the front door, slammed it behind me and yelled, "Marie, I'm home."

There was some scurrying and whispering upstairs, then she called, "You're home early. I'm just about to take a shower and then I'll be down."

"Is there anything I can do for you, Brad?" Rob asked as he walked calmly down the stairs a moment later. Calmly? Robots had only one expression and no body language, although Robots, Inc., was making improvements with each successive model.

"Not right now, Rob," I said. "Maybe you could get started with dinner." He always served dinner at exactly six-thirty.

"Of course," he said and strode toward the kitchen.

I flopped onto the sofa and thought about everything. I'd wanted to watch. I'd wanted to see my wife fucking another man for years, but I hadn't ever dared mention it to her, nor did I think I could deal with my jealousy. Now I had the perfect solution. Rob wasn't "another man." He was a robot. Watching him fuck Marie wouldn't bother me at all.

We spent the evening as though nothing had happened. As we prepared for bed, I said, "It was nice being home early together today. Are you making it an early day any other time this week?"

"Actually, I thought I'd come home early Thursday." There was a slight hesitation in her voice as she asked, "Can you get off too?"

"Not a chance," I said, knowing I'd arrange to be home at all costs. "I have a big meeting with the Danforth folks about the new contract . . ." Stop babbling.

Marie seemed to sigh and look a bit relieved. "Oh, I'm so sorry. It would have been fun."

It will be, I thought.

Thursday, I left work at one, pleading a stomach virus. Actually, my cock was so hard at the prospect of watching Rob and Marie that I hurt a lot, but slightly below my stomach. I hurried home, parked on the next block and, while Rob was at the market, slipped into the house and onto the second-floor porch. I cracked the sliding door to our bedroom so I could hear whatever went on, then stretched out on a lounge chair and waited. At about four, I became aware of noises on the stairs. I moved to the edge of the sliding door and peeped into the bedroom. Rob and Marie were just entering.

"Let's do scenario number seven," Marie said.

"As you wish." Rob turned on some music and stripped to the waist. God, I thought, he's got some gorgeous body. Robotics, Inc., sure knows its stuff. Then Rob walked to Marie and slowly unfastened her blouse and bra, throwing them to one side until her beautiful breasts were bared. I couldn't help notice that her nipples were already hard and her skin was flushed a deep rosy pink.

Rob wrapped his arms around her, and they began to slow dance, every move fluid, body rubbing against body. Marie smiled and sighed as Rob began to kiss her neck and jaw, his mouth slowly making its way to her lips. The kiss was long and deep. It's been a while since we've kissed that way, I thought, as I watched Marie sway and rub her pubic bone against Rob's lower body. No hard-on there, I thought, somewhat relieved, and curious about what they would do without a hard cock to consummate the afternoon's activities.

As I watched, Rob placed his hand beneath Marie's arms and effortlessly lifted her until her deep brown nipples were level with his mouth. Holding her in the air, he sucked one into his mouth, and I couldn't miss the slurping sounds. Marie's head fell back, and there was an expression of supreme pleasure on her face.

Slowly Rob walked to the bed and lay Marie on it, his mouth never leaving her nipple. He pulled off the remainder of her clothing and spread her legs as he kissed and licked his way down her belly. The scene was so erotic that I found my hand sliding my zipper down and pulling out my own hard cock.

As I watched, Rob's mouth moved between my wife's legs, and he began to pleasure her. God, I thought, it's been forever since I've done that for her. No wonder she turned to the robot. And, judging from her whimpering and moaning, she's trained him perfectly. I used to be able to give her that.

I found it wasn't jealousy driving me, but envy. I didn't begrudge her her pleasures, but I wanted to be the one to give them to her. I wanted to pull Rob away and plunge my now-rock-hard cock into her sweet pussy. How long had it been?

Minutes passed, and suddenly I was willing to risk everything. I slid the door open and, as Rob sat back on his haunches to use his fingers to further please Marie, I waved him away. I found my wife's pussy hot and wet, dripping with her juices. I explored, the way I had done so many times early on in our marriage. I reveled in her tiny squeaks and groans as I found places I'd forgotten but she hadn't. Then I found her clit and rubbed it ever so gently, watching her hips buck and her fists clench.

I tasted her. Her eyes tightly shut, she still hadn't noticed that I wasn't Rob. Well, soon she would. I licked and sucked until I thought that neither of us could wait any longer, then moved until I could plunge my cock into her. I felt her go rigid and saw her eyes fly open.

"I thought," she said, barely able to breathe, "it was Rob doing a better imitation of you than ever." She gasped as I withdrew and plunged in again. "I trained him to perform exactly as you used to." As I plunged again, she grabbed my ass cheeks and dug her nails into my flesh. "God, I do prefer the real thing." As I withdrew, Marie grabbed my now-slippery cock and pulled me back. "I prefer you. Oh, God, Brad, do it. Fuck me so hard, so fast!" She fell back, and I climbed over her, pounding my cock into her harder and harder, until the entire room reverberated with the sounds of our screams.

I think we dozed, and awoke to make love again. It must have been more than two hours later when I heard a voice from the doorway. "It's almost a quarter of seven. Your dinner is getting cold," he said. Did he sound just a bit irritated?

We laughed, pulled on a few clothes and walked down the stairs. I'd learned quite a lot that day. "Do me a favor," I said. "Any time you have the urge for an afternoon delight, call me."

"You bet," Marie said. Then added with a wink, "Although, if Rob were anatomically correct . . ."

I swatted her behind . . . and wondered.

# Naked Places

"You want me to do what?" Lisa said, staring at the slick color photo in the men's magazine that her husband brandished.

"I didn't say I wanted you to do anything," Josh replied. "I merely said that I think this woman with her pussy shaved is really hot."

"I can't imagine why," Lisa said, her heart pounding. Josh had often suggested new things for the bedroom, and they had tried and enjoyed dildos, blindfolds and a few other things he'd mentioned over the years, but this was going too far.

"I would think it's obvious," Josh said, turning the magazine back so he could gaze at the woman's picture. "I can see everything. If I were making love to her, I could see her lips swell as she got hot. It would be dynamite." As Lisa took a deep breath to protest, he held up his hand. "Hey, don't make such a fuss. I didn't mean you have to shave. I just think it's really hot." He rubbed the growing bulge in his jeans. "Makes me hard just thinking about it."

Lisa said nothing, and eventually he went back to his reading. Over the next few days, however, Lisa's mind kept returning to that picture. She knew that women were shaved before childbirth and had heard that it was itchy as it grew out, but that wasn't what deterred her. It seemed so slutty, somehow. Slutty. The word kept echoing in her brain. Slutty. Maybe she *could* do it. She remembered the heated look in Josh's eyes as he gazed at the picture. And she knew that, although he'd never insist on something she found a turn-off, he was suggesting that she do it.

While her husband was off running some Saturday errands, Lisa logged on to the Internet and brought up her favorite search engine. She typed "genital shaving" and found dozens of pages devoted to it. Many were just photos of women with hairless pussies, but some had real information on how to go about it. She printed out a few pages of advice, then logged off.

Over and over, she read the advice. Then, at the bottom of a page, she found a short sentence: "It can be more fun if you let your partner shave you." Maybe she could do that. She hid the pages in the bathroom closet, then went to the large drugstore in town and picked up a ladies' razor, a small pair of sharp scissors, some lightly scented shaving cream and a bottle of witch hazel, which one site recommended for afterward. She'd do it. They'd do it. Tonight.

That evening, they settled down to watch a movie Josh had rented, but Lisa found that she couldn't concentrate. She felt the Internet pages and the small bag of implements calling her. Finally, unable to wait any longer, she hastened into the bathroom, got the papers, then returned to the living room and flipped off the DVD player. She put the sheets on the table beside Josh's lounge chair, straddled his lap and dropped onto his thighs. Trying to sound confident of her decision, she said, "I've been thinking about that picture you showed me a few days ago."

"What picture?" he asked.

"Don't be like that. You know what picture. The center-fold with the hairless crotch."

Josh unsuccessfully tried to hide a grin. "Oh, that," he said with mock innocence.

"Yeah, that."

"And . . ."

"You know me well enough to realize that I'd know you were suggesting that I shave." She paused, then took a deep breath. "I got some information from the Web and, well . . ." She felt suddenly reluctant to continue.

Josh reached between her jeans-covered thighs and patted her crotch. "You did it?" He grinned as widely as he ever had. "I'm flabbergasted."

"Well, I didn't exactly," she said, a bit hesitant. Would he go for it? "Well, I thought you could do it for me."

Suddenly his eyes darkened and passion thickened his voice. "You mean it?"

Emboldened by his expression, Lisa said, "I mean it."

"Right now?"

"Right now." She handed him the pages and watched while he scanned the printed words.

"We'll need a few things," Josh said.

"I got them today." Lisa placed her hand in her husband's lap, and when she felt the hard ridge of him, she knew she'd made the right decision. "Let me take a quick shower, and then we can start." As she headed for the bathroom, she saw him rereading the pages she had given him.

She took a short shower, washing carefully between her legs. Then, when she was done, she wrapped a towel around her sarong style, and she opened the bathroom door. While she had been in the shower, Josh had been busy. Several large towels covered the bed, and he had all the items she had bought laid out on the bedside table. "You still okay with this?" he asked.

"I think I am."

"Well," Josh said, smiling, "if we don't like it, it will grow back."

"Yeah, but I gather that's not too comfortable."

"Whatever happens, I'll kiss it every morning to make it better."

Lisa grinned. It would be all right. She stretched out on the bed, and Josh arranged her body in a position that was comfortable yet easy for him to get at, her feet on the floor, her legs spread. First, he clipped the hair really short. The snip-snip of the scissors was sort of sexy, but Lisa had to smile at the look of total concentration on her husband's face. Finally he looked up, then leered and pressed the cold scissors against her heated flesh. "Whoa!" she yelled. "Don't make me jump."

He chuckled, then said, "You know I wouldn't do it at a bad moment." Josh went into the bathroom, then returned with a pot of warm water and the can of shaving cream. Slowly, almost erotically, he spread thick foam over Lisa's pussy, making a great show of covering every inch.

Lisa could feel her body begin to respond to his ministrations. "I don't think you're supposed to be arousing me."

"Why in the world not?" Josh said, now obviously stroking her.

"I don't know. Won't it make it more difficult?"

"I wouldn't think so," he said, still playing with her. Finally, when she wanted to just fuck his brains out and forget about the shaving part, he said, "Let's do it. Still okay?"

"Yes," she whispered, now quite turned on and ready for anything. She felt the razor slowly slide over her skin, finding all her folds and crevasses. She shivered, but she kept her body completely still, worried about possible nicks and scratches. Eventually Josh pronounced the job done, and he washed her with warm water.

Suddenly she could concentrate on the nakedness between her legs. The feeling was amazing. Skin was cool where cool had never been before. Sweet, soft air flowed over her most intimate parts. Josh sat between her legs and just stared, then leaned down and blew a stream of cool air over her. God, she was getting hot. Just the feel of his eyes on her was making her nipples pucker and her tissues swell and moisten. "I can see you getting wet," Josh said. "I can watch your clit swell and your lips open. This is so incredible." He touched her lightly here, then there, tapping and probing. Then he rose, and took some cotton balls and wet them with the witch hazel, and slowly, ever so slowly, stroked her skin over and over as the sensations drove her higher. He rubbed, then blew cool air, and repeated the motions, until she thought she'd explode. She wanted to move her hips, but she held perfectly still as her husband stared at her.

Then one finger was at her opening, pressing just slightly inside. "This isn't hurting you, is it?" he asked.

"No." She could barely get the word out.

Then two fingers were inside her, slowly spreading her open while Josh watched, enthralled. "I've never seen it this way before. So open, ready, available." Then he was as naked as she, her towel open, her body exposed in a way she'd never been before. He knelt on the floor between her knees and rubbed his cock over her now-smooth skin. Over and over he delved into her, then withdrew, again to stroke, tease and watch. "It's difficult to hold back," he said, "but I want to see it all."

She felt the tip of his tongue flick over her clit. "This tastes a bit strange, but most of the witch hazel has evaporated," he said, almost clinically. He licked again, his tongue slowly sliding over her newly smooth skin and into the folds of her vaginal flesh. "You taste hot," he said, sticking the point of his tongue into her. "Hot and so very wet and sweet. It's difficult to wait any longer. Do you want me?"

What a ridiculous question, she thought. "God, yes."

Then his cock was deep inside of her, and she wrapped her legs around his waist, holding him tightly inside her. She squeezed her vaginal muscles, and she knew he could keep himself still no longer. Suddenly he pounded into her, and in only a few seconds, he came. Then he pulled back and rubbed her clit in the way he knew would bring her to orgasm quickly. And it did. Unable to get her breath, she came, several of his fingers inside her, others teasing and massaging every inch of her.

Lying side by side, they dozed, then showered again. Afterward, Josh again bathed her in witch hazel, and naked, they slipped between the cool sheets. During the night, every time Lisa turned, she was aware of the naked feeling between her legs. She knew that she'd be as hot when she awoke as she had been earlier, and Josh would be only too eager to oblige. Would she be itchy and stuff later? Who knew? Who cared?

# *Tarzan*

Okay, you're going to laugh, but I have a Tarzan fetish. Here's my fantasy.

Tarzan is about eighteen in my dream. I know it shouldn't matter, but I want to make him old enough so I don't have any lingering hesitation about doing it with an underage guy. He's never done it with anyone before. A virgin.

I was captured by some really bad guys, and he rescued me. During my escape, I turned my ankle, so now I'm in Tarzan's tree house, my ankle supported on some pine-needle pillows. Don't get picky on me now and tell me there aren't any pine trees in a jungle. It's my fantasy, so I can have whatever I want.

The air smells of damp earth, trees and jungle flowers. I can hear rushing water from a stream nearby and, above that, the roar of leopards and the trumpeting of elephants. He's left a cup of clear water beside me, and I take a sip, feeling the icy liquid on my tongue.

My clothing is torn, like Jane's in the movie. Tarzan is out right now, preparing food for both of us. Let me describe him before I go any further. I've always loved tall men, so he's about six two. His body is all muscle, with great thighs and six-pack abs. His shoulders are wide, and he's got the greatest upper arms you've ever seen, like those of professional basketball players.

His hair is black, and he wears it long, tied back with a strip of leather, and I guess he's handsome. I can't say for sure because I really don't see his face at any time in my fantasy. I suppose I really don't care.

He arrives back at the tree house with fruit and cooked fish. We eat in silence. Actually, he hasn't said a word. Maybe he hasn't learned to speak to anyone but animals. We eat slowly. I savor each mouthful because I know what's going to happen. He doesn't, yet.

He watches me, my hands, my arms, my feet, my long legs, revealed through the tatters of my skirt. But he especially watches my breasts. I guess he has never seen a woman's breasts before. Most of the buttons on my shirt are missing, so when I move, he gets a view of the lacy edges of my bra. He can't seem to take his eyes off of it.

Enjoying my teasing, I keep shifting position, and eventually I let my thighs part so he can look up my skirt. Is he curious? You bet. Still there are no words.

I finish my food and put the crude wooden plate aside. When he puts his down, I see that he hasn't eaten a thing. I fix my eyes on his and slowly unbutton one of the only two buttons left on my blouse. Then I slide my fingers over my skin and deep into my cleavage. Now he's torn, watching my eyes and my fingers. I look at his loincloth and see his erection pushing against the animal skin he wears.

Oh, yes, this is going to be wonderful. The second button is open now, and I part the sides of the blouse. Most of my bra is beige satin, except for the centers of the cups, which are matching lace, allowing my nipples to show through the sheer fabric. Tarzan stares. He's sitting only a foot away from me, so I reach forward and take his hand. I put it on the soft breast flesh above the cup. I use his fingers to stroke my chest around my bra. I savor the expectation, not wanting to rush.

As I look down, I love the contrast between his deeply tanned hands and my soft beige bra and white skin. He's staring at my breasts, his eyes hot. Does he know what's going to happen? He's never seen a woman before, but he's seen animals, I'm sure, so what can he be imagining?

The pads of his fingers are rough as they scrape over my skin, and my nipples pucker as he watches. He looks up, a question in his eyes, and I nod. He strokes over the soft fabric of one cup until his fingers reach my swollen nub. It's difficult for me to allow things to progress slowly now, but I force myself.

Soon the fingers of his other hand are fondling my other breast, and I can feel the wetness soaking my panties. With trembling hands, I take the bra off, and his fingers find my naked breasts. He's curious, rubbing, pulling at my nipple, pinching. I cup the back of his head and guide his mouth to my hungry tit. He wastes no time. He licks, tasting my skin. He suckles, each suck slashing directly to my pussy. I'm so hot, I think I can come right then, but I hold myself tightly in check. I can barely catch my breath, and my pulse is throbbing through me, but still I wait.

Long minutes go by as I revel in the sensations caused by his rough hands. Then I reach out and slide my palms over his chest, now lightly sweat-dampened. I spend as long as I want teasing the palms of my hands with his deeply tanned skin and the rigid muscles beneath. I can see his cock twitch below the minuscule skin covering him. Just wait. There's so much more.

I take his hands and hold them to one side, then pull off the rest of my clothes. Naked now, I settle back in my chair and watch Tarzan's eyes roam from my breasts to the hair between my legs. I know he wants to touch me there, but he's hesitant. I nod, then take one of his hands and put it on my belly and slide it lower. I part my thighs so he can explore to his heart's content.

His callused fingers find my wet core, ignoring my clit. He has no idea that it matters. Part of me wants to guide his fingers to my clit, but I know that if he touches me there, I'll climax too quickly. He delves into my folds and finally finds my opening.

I urge him to push his fingers inside of me, and he does, filling me more completely than I've ever been filled. I can't take too much, so I soon move his hands away and pull off his covering, revealing his huge, hard cock, now fully erect. I hold it in my hand, then wrap my fingers around it. I can barely contain it all. I cup his heavy testicles, and he gasps.

I don't dare play with him any more because I know he's as close to coming as I am, so I show him that I want him to put his cock into me. He does, hard, fast. I cup his muscular buttocks and use my hips to tell him just how I want to be fucked. And fuck me he does, until I come for the first time. He's got the stamina of a bull and lasts longer than I had thought he might, thrusting and withdrawing until I come again, and again, screaming.

Eventually, however, he arches his back and groans, spurting into me, pulling me with him for one last orgasm.

I love this fantasy, and usually I masturbate to several orgasms while dreaming about my jungle and my Tarzan. Then I fall asleep, totally satisfied.

# A Visit to the Doctor

Like most people, I have fantasies. Mind you, I have no intention of ever acting them out, but when I dream them, in the dark of night, I live them.

I'm a doctor, pretty, petite, very bosomy, as I always am in my dreams. I have to give a physical to a hunky new male patient, a Mr. Montgomery. After I take a history, I tell him to go into the exam room, strip and put on the little cotton gown that he'll find in there. He disappears. I really don't have any unprofessional thoughts. Yet.

In the exam room, I notice that he's really gorgeous, with tight abs, wonderful buns, which I see beneath the silly gown when he briefly turns his back to me, great legs and arms. I hardly notice his face. While he sits on the exam table, I take his blood pressure and listen to his heart and breathing, chatting aimlessly, keeping it completely professional. Now it's time for me to examine his genitals and prostate, so I have him lie back on the table. Is this the way it's done in real life? I've no idea, but it's my fantasy, so I can do it whatever way I want.

First I cup his heavy balls, testing the weight and balance. Both are of equal size, and there's nothing out of the ordinary. I must admit that I love men's genitals—the feel, the smell, the taste—but I'm getting ahead of myself.

Now I have to feel his cock. I notice that it's swelling slightly, and I suspect he must be quite embarrassed. "It's okay if you feel some sexual pleasure," I say. "It's natural. I'll try to be completely neutral about it all." I'm not, actually. He's so beautiful, and as I watch his cock twitch, my pussy gets wet. God, I'd love to fuck his brains out, but, after all, I'm a doctor. I smile slightly. The hell with professionalism. I'm going to enjoy myself.

"I need to check your genitals for abnormalities," I say, grasping his cock and squeezing. It's getting harder, and he's looking quite disquieted, and maybe a little amused.

"It's okay. Do your worst," he says.

My worst? I squeeze again, and now his cock is about half-erect. I love the fact that my hands can do that. I cup his balls in the other hand and slowly stroke his cock from base to tip. I can hear his long sigh as he raises his knees and adjusts his hips on the table.

His cock grows as I stroke. When I can tear my gaze away from his beautiful member, I look into his eyes and find him staring at me, his lids half-closed. He licks his lips. I keep stroking. "I like what you're doing," he says.

"I like it too," I whisper as I manipulate his cock and balls. He's fully erect now, but I'm not ready for him to come. "I need to check your prostate." He looks wary. "It's really important," I say. For me, and for you. "Have you ever had a thorough prostate exam before?"

"No," he says.

"Trust me," I say. "It won't hurt." I lower my voice. "Quite the opposite, actually," I murmur. Slowly, with his eyes watching intently, I put on a pair of latex gloves, smoothing the white plastic over each finger. As he watches me, his cock moves of its own volition. He's aroused and hungry for more.

When my gloves are on, I squeeze a large dollop of lubricating gel onto my fingers and rub it over his anus. "This won't hurt," I say again. "Just relax." I press my index finger against his opening and place the palm of my other hand on his lower abdomen. I can feel his muscles contract, reflexively trying to keep my finger out. They can't, and slowly my finger penetrates his rear opening. Gradually I push deeper, and his cock leaps to attention, growing as hard as it can.

With my finger deep inside his ass, I lick my lips and take his cock into my mouth. I keep thrusting in and out of his ass while I suck deeply, then withdraw from his cock. I coordinate my movements so I pull out of his ass as I suck his cock into my mouth. He's being penetrated or penetrating with each stroke. Soon, he can wait no longer, and I feel small contractions deep in his anus. Then my mouth fills with his come.

I'm in my bed, with my fingers working in my crotch. As he comes in my fantasy, I come in reality. It's such a powerful dream that it makes me come every time. God, I love my fantasy lovers.

# Beads

Val had found them at a garage sale. Of course, they were just ordinary-sized beads, but the set was so intriguing that she just had to have them, and they were only ten dollars. Gold colored, there was one long strand and several shorter ones of varying lengths, which could be worn separately or connected to make one long strand that would hang almost to her feet. She knew that in different combinations, they could be almost any length. Such fun, and such a wonderful addition to her funky wardrobe.

When she got them home, she connected and reconnected them, marveling at the ingenious clasps, strong yet almost invisible. When Bret arrived home, she called her husband into the bedroom. "Aren't these clever?" she said. "Look how they clip together."

"Those are really nice, Val. Maybe you should wear them to Marge and Tom's party tomorrow night."

"Great idea. How about my red dress? They would look really good with it." And drive Bret crazy. He always liked that dress, and it had made him horny enough the last time she'd worn it that he'd run to the bedroom and thrown her on the bed when they got home. "Yeah, the red dress."

The following evening, she washed the beads in soapy

water and watched them get still shinier. Then she attached just the right ones so the strand would fall into her cleavage. She was finally dressed when Bret came out of the bathroom, a small package in his hands.

"I love those beads and had a kinky idea," he said. He handed her the small box.

Inside lay a long, thick gold chain. "I got it at one of those mall kiosks, and I think it will be just the right length," he said.

Bret stopped her as she started to fasten the long chain around her neck. "Not that way," he said. "Where are the rest of those beads?"

She motioned toward the bathroom vanity. What did he have in mind? she wondered.

He got the strands and selected one about a foot long. "Pull up your skirt," he said.

Never one to underestimate his delicious mind, Val lifted the soft, full skirt of the dress. "What are you doing?" she asked.

"You'll see."

She felt the cool chain as he looped it around her waist and let it rest just above her hips. Then she felt him hook the beads to the front of the chain, and pull the strand between her legs and clip it to the back of the chain. "Shit," she said, "that's cold."

"Not for long," he said. "Your pussy will keep it *just* right."

As she stood, the beads warmed.

"Let's see what happens when you walk around," Bret said.

She took a few steps toward the bathroom and felt her inner lips rub gently against the smooth surface of the beads.

"Is that as kinky as I thought it would be?" Bret asked.

Damn, she thought. "It's really bad," she said. Her grin said that "bad" was a good thing.

Afraid that her little harness would show beneath the soft skirt, she walked slowly into the bathroom and gazed in the mirror. Nothing showed below, but the beads around her neck took on a different significance. As they rubbed against her skin, she was continually reminded, even standing totally still, of the ones buried between her legs. This was going to be quite an evening.

"And no cheating and taking them off in the ladies' room," Bret said. "Scouts' honor."

"Scouts' honor," Val answered. Suddenly she had an idea. She looked at the remaining lengths of necklace, grabbed one and said, "Two can play at this game. Drop your pants."

Grinning, Bret unfastened his belt and let his slacks fall to the floor. Then he thumbed his shorts, and they fell as well. He was almost embarrassed at how hard his cock was.

"Not right now," Val said. "But let's put your mind where mine is." She quickly hooked the strand around his balls and the base of his cock, like a cock ring. It wouldn't impede his blood flow, and soon his cock would soften, but it would be there and he'd feel it. She hoped it was tight enough not to fall off. "Just keep that there," she said, patting his cock. "Scouts' honor."

"Scouts' honor," he said with a grin as he pulled on his shorts and slacks.

As they drove to their friends' house, both were quiet, focused on what they felt between their legs. As the evening progressed, Val found she could actually forget about the beads for a few minutes, then she'd move and be erotically reminded. She would glance over at Bret then, and their matching grins would be difficult to hide.

At one point, Val's friend Marge asked about the hot

looks between her and her husband. "Something kinky I might tell you about some day," Val answered.

"Secrets, girl? Not fair. Especially the perverse ones. Give."

"Not tonight," Val said. "There isn't time. Actually, I think Bret and I will be leaving early." She nodded at Bret and motioned toward the door. "Like right now."

"Have at it, girl, but promise to tell me tomorrow. First thing."

"Done."

She met Bret at the door, and they rushed to their car. "I don't think we'll make it home," Val panted. "I want to rip your clothes off right here in Marge and Tom's driveway."

"Me too. I never imagined this thing would work the way it has, but I'm so hot, I think I'll explode."

The drive home was short but still too long for the silent pair. Val's pussy was twitching, and her juices had already soaked her panties. She could tell from the quite obvious bulge in Bret's pants that he was just as impatient as she was. They drove into their driveway, but Bret didn't pull the car into the garage. "Right here," he said, turning the engine off and flipping off the lights.

"But the neighbors . . ."

"It's dark, and they should all be in watching the news anyway. And if they see something, fuck them," he growled.

Val reached behind her and unzipped her dress. "How about fucking me instead."

Bret pulled his polo shirt over his head, revealing his smooth, sexy chest. Val couldn't decide whether to continue trying to get her dress off over her head or slide her hands over his skin. Her need to touch him won out, and she splayed her hands over his chest, rubbing her palms over his nipples. While she stroked, her head fell back and her breathing quickened.

Bret pulled off his belt, unfastened his pants and wiggled out of them, then unsnapped Val's bra, freeing her needy breasts. She felt him pull her dress down to her waist while he lowered his mouth to her nipples. His sucking drove her wild with need, and she lifted her behind, and dragged her dress and panties off and tossed them into the backseat. As she settled back down, she felt the beads nestled in her wetness and was reminded of Bret's.

She reached beneath the waistband of his shorts and grabbed the strand of beads, now fastened tightly around his "package," holding his balls and cock away from his body. "God, you're so big," she purred.

He quickly pulled his shorts off, then grabbed the chain that connected to her love beads. He slid them back and forth over her lips and clit, bringing her closer to orgasm. My God, she thought, I'm going to come right here, where any of the neighbors might see. Well, she reasoned, if she was going to come, he was too. She wrapped her hand around his cock, already slippery from the semen dripping from the tip, and began to slide it up and down, enjoying the length of him.

"Keep doing that, and I'm going to come before I'm even inside you," he said, his voice hoarse and shaky.

"Just don't stop what you're doing," she said, barely able to drag enough air into her lungs to make a sound.

His fingers joined the beads, rubbing her clit until she was unable to stop the spasms. "Oh, oh, oh," she said, her head falling back against the headrest, her hands still working in Bret's groin. Panting, she grinned at him, then winked. "Tit for tat," she said. wiggling around the gearshift lever and sucking him into her mouth. She groped for his hands and filled them with her breasts, then pulled her head back, still maintaining suction on his cock. Back, then down again, over and over. It only took a few sucks for him to fill her mouth with his come, his low growl echoing through the closed car.

"My God," he said, minutes later when they had both caught their breath. "My God. That was amazing."

"Pull this car into the garage, and we can finish this upstairs."

"Finish? You mean there's more?"

"Upstairs, lover. Then we'll find out."

# *Puss in Boots*

Carl was six feet tall and built like an athlete. He worked out three times a week to keep his body in shape, and liked the way his smooth skin was stretched taut over a well-muscled body. The combination of his curly blond hair and deep brown eyes seemed to make him irresistible, and he dated a different woman just about every weekend.

One Saturday evening, Carl was attending a party at a friend's house. The wine and booze flowed freely, and everyone was feeling quite mellow. He had noticed several attractive women, but he was willing to circulate, to bide his time.

As Carl wandered toward the makeshift bar, he spotted her. It was not unusual that he noticed her. She was striking. But the instant excitement that he felt surprised him. He liked his women short and stacked. This woman was tall, almost five feet ten, and had red hair that hung almost to her waist. Her body was firm and trim, with small breasts. Not his usual type at all. And she wasn't wearing the uniform of the evening either—the slinky dress that advertised. Instead, she was wearing a black blouse buttoned up to her throat and tied at the waist, and tight, black stretch pants. She had accentuated her waist with a silver concha belt, which matched the large, silver squash-blossom earrings she was wearing. She completed her outfit with knee-high black leather boots.

Carl forgot about drinks and started toward the girl. As he got closer, he admired her green eyes and smooth skin. He gazed at her red lips and felt a further tightening in his pants.

"Hi, gorgeous," he said, using his most charming voice. "How about I get you a fresh drink, and then we can get to know each other?"

The girl looked at him. Her eyes roamed over his body, making him a bit self-conscious. Then she looked away. A challenge. That was good. He was going to enjoy this. "I'm sorry," he said, "are you with someone?"

"No," she said with her back to him.

"Then why not me?"

"You're not my type," she said.

Carl was amazed. He was used to having women fall all over him. "And what is your type?" Carl asked.

She turned and looked at him. "My type always waits for me to make the first move. As a matter of fact, my type always waits for me to make every move."

He was suddenly painfully hard. His whole body shuddered, and he could hardly control his excitement. His pulse hammered in his neck, and his breathing quickened. He could hardly get the words out. "What would your type do right now?" he stammered.

She gazed into his eyes, then let a smile gradually spread over her face. "My type would get a glass of white wine from the bar and bring it to me."

Carl hurried to the bar and grabbed an already-poured wine, then hustled back to where the woman was standing. He handed the glass to her with shaking hands.

"Hmm," she said. "Very good." Then she wandered off through the crowd.

He stood rooted to the spot. He had never had an experience like this one, and he was not going to let it end.

He stood in the same spot for almost an hour, until finally the girl returned. He looked at her and smiled his most seductive smile. She stood close to him. "Never look me in the eye," she said sternly. "You may look at me only from the shoulders down, unless I give you permission. Understand?"

Carl looked at her boots. They were shiny, with pointed toes, silver toe tips, heavy silver rings through the zippers and high spike heels. "Yes, I understand." He could hardly speak.

"My name is Valerie. You should learn to say, 'Yes, Valerie.' Now practice that."

"Yes, Valerie," Carl said.

"Not bad for a beginner," she said. As she spoke, all Carl could see were her hands, long red fingernails sliding up and down the hips of her tight pants. "Now we go into the bathroom," she said. Her voice was soft but firm, and seemed to brook no objections. "Take off your shorts and bring them to me."

Carl almost ran into the bathroom. He pulled off his slacks and briefs, freeing his huge erection to poke from his crotch. Then he pulled his slacks back on. He caught some of his pubic hair in the zipper in his haste to return to Valerie and fumbled with shaking hands to free it.

He left the bathroom, his shorts balled in one hand, and hurried back through the crowd. He found her where he had left her, standing beside the fireplace. He remembered and lowered his eyes so he gazed at her boots as he surreptitiously handed her his shorts. Valerie propped her elbow on the mantel as she dangled his shorts from her index finger for all to see. There were several snickers from other people at the party, but Carl was willing to risk anything. Why? He hadn't a clue. All he knew was that he was more turned on than he ever remembered being. He started to reach for the shorts, but Valerie glared at him. He dropped his hand and blushed for the first time, lowering his eyes to her leather boots.

"I see we understand each other," she said, a smile in her voice. "Go and find my coat. It's a long black leather jacket. Bring it to me, and we'll get out of here."

Carl went into the bedroom and rooted through the coats, finding her jacket toward the bottom. He wondered again why he was doing this. Had this girl cast some kind of spell over him? She had, and he knew what it was. He had to have her. He would do anything she wanted just to get a chance to make love to her.

Later, in a cab on the way to her apartment, she said, "Give me your wrists." She rummaged around in her purse and pulled out a length of soft black rope. He offered her his wrists, and she tied them together, then reached down and lifted one heavy silver ring attached to her boot. Ever so slowly, she took one end of the rope and tied it to the ring.

When they reached their destination, the rope forced Carl to get out of the taxi carefully and walk slightly bent over, with his head level with her breasts. Twice, he almost stumbled when Valerie took a particularly long step. When he regained his balance, she laughed.

There was another couple in the elevator as they took it to the eighth floor, and he tried to look the other way and ignore their incredulous stares. He didn't care what anyone thought. He wanted, needed, whatever was to come.

He followed Valerie into her apartment, and she turned on the lights. All the furniture was chrome, glass or black lacquer. The rug was dark red with deep pile, and it silenced their footsteps. Silently, she untied the end of the rope attached to her boot and retied it to a ring imbedded in the wall. Then she turned and disappeared into the next room.

It was very warm in her apartment. Carl, still wearing his outdoor jacket, began to sweat. He felt a trickle of perspiration run down his side. He wiggled as much as he could, trying to brush his shirt against the tiny river.

"Don't squirm," she said as she reentered the room. He gazed at her. She had changed into a black corset and long black gloves without fingers. She had pulled her hair back tightly and wound it into a tight knot at the back of her neck. She still wore her boots and was banging a short riding crop against the top of one.

She swished the crop against the backs of Carl's thighs. The effect was muffled by his slacks, but the crop still stung. "You were looking at me," she snapped. Carl immediately dropped his gaze.

Valerie reached up and untied Carl's hands. As she stretched, one naked breast brushed against Carl's face. He shuddered. He wondered how much of this he could take before he came in his pants.

Valerie walked over to the sofa and sat down, the rope still in her hands. "Strip," she ordered. Carl obeyed as quickly as he could with his hands shaking as hard as they were.

Now he stood before her naked. He knew she was looking him over, and he was proud of his well-developed physique. He was also proud of the size of his erection as it poked straight in front of him, aching for relief.

"Not bad," she said, then continued, "but I don't care much for size. I demand stamina from my men. You may not come unless I tell you to. The first time is always the most difficult, so I will give you some help. Come over here." Carl walked closer. "Now touch yourself."

Carl had never masturbated with anyone watching. When he hesitated, the crop swished through the air and landed on his right ass cheek. He knew that there was now a bright red line. He reached out and wrapped his hand around his throbbing erection.

"Stroke it until you come," she said. "Then you can serve me properly." She settled back to watch.

Carl was very embarrassed but also incredibly excited. He squeezed his cock and ran his hand up and down it. It was only a minute until he spurted all over her legs.

"You made a mess," she said. "Clean it up!"

Carl started to look around for a towel.

"With your tongue!"

He hesitated only a second, then licked up all his juice. He would do anything she wanted. When he was finished, she picked up four ropes from an end table and tied one to each ankle and wrist. Then she took a blindfold and covered his eyes. It was a new sensation for Carl. He was in darkness, unaware of what was happening around him. He listened to every sound, trying to figure out exactly what Valerie was doing.

She pushed him down on the floor and tied each of the ropes to a piece of furniture so he was spread-eagled, face-up, on the soft carpet. He tried to pull on each of the ropes, but he soon discovered that he was completely helpless.

He felt her soft fingers exploring his face around the blindfold. She stroked his forehead and his cheeks. She inserted a fingernail into each ear, pressing in and out as if she were fucking his ears with her fingers. Then she stroked his lips. His mouth opened, and she fucked it with her fingers. His cock was rock hard again. "I enjoy watching my men use their mouth. Sucking correctly is an important part of satisfying a woman."

She continued to fuck his mouth with her fingers, feeling him sucking. Then she leaned over and put her nipple in his mouth. "Suck good," she said.

He sucked on her nipple, varying the pressure of his mouth. First he sucked hard, pulling her deeply into his mouth. Then he suckled gently, like a baby. Then he drew her nipple into his mouth again and bit.

She slapped him across the face. "No teeth unless I say so." He continued to suck, listening to her begin to purr. "That's much better," she said. "You are very talented with your mouth."

She pulled away. "Now suck this."

It was soft, jelly-like plastic. A dildo. He sucked it, hard, making slurping sounds. She spent a long time watching as he sucked the dildo she was using to fuck his mouth. In and out it slid.

Suddenly she pulled the dildo out and straddled his face. He could see nothing around the blindfold, but he smelled her juices. He licked his lips as she lowered her pussy. He lapped at her soaking cunt, flicking his tongue across her clit. He pushed his tongue into her as deep as it would go, then pulled it out and slid it across her swollen, hot clit.

He licked and sucked until he felt her muscles tighten and then spasm. As her muscles worked, he used their rhythm to determine the rhythm of his tongue. She ground her pelvis against his face as she came, crying, "Very, very good!"

She collapsed onto Carl's chest, panting. They lay together while her breathing subsided. Then she said, "You did very well, for a beginner. Now you get your reward."

Still blindfolded, Carl could only feel what was happening. Valerie climbed off of him, and there were rustling sounds. Suddenly, Carl felt her mouth around his cock. She sucked on him the way he had sucked on the dildo. There was something especially erotic about her sucking the same way he had done just minutes before. It took only moments for him to spill his load into her mouth.

Later she untied him, and they fucked again, this time in her bed.

Carl now sees Valerie three or four times a month. Each of them has other lovers, of course. This wasn't love, just satisfaction of mutual need. But satisfy each other they do. Explosively.

# Something Naughty

"**D**id you do anything naughty today?" my husband asked with a leer as he arrived home from work one Tuesday evening. Hearing those words made my knees shake, my pussy swell and my fluids flow. That's the phrase that lets me know he's interested in playing one of our favorite role-playing games.

Let me explain, so you don't get the wrong idea. There's a lot of spousal abuse around, but this definitely isn't among it. Several months ago, we jointly discovered my love of being "punished" and Gary's love of "punishing" me. It began with a slap on my ass while making love and sort of grew from there. Now we play this particular game once a month or so. My mind scrambled for something I could tell him, some monstrous thing I had done that day that would be worthy of punishment. "I-I-I charged a new sweater on your charge card without permission," I said, feeling almost guilty. Of course, I hadn't bought anything in several weeks, and if I had, it wouldn't be a problem. However, I needed an evil deed, and that was the best I could come up with on short notice. And it didn't really matter anyway.

"That was very naughty," Gary said, putting his briefcase on the floor by the front door and slowly scratching his palm as if itching to spank my bottom. I could feel my nipples swell and my heart pound.

"I'm really sorry, you know. I really don't need to be punished. Really." I tend to repeat myself when I'm excited, and Gary knows it.

"I know you don't think you do, but I have to teach you a lesson. For your own good, of course."

Getting fully into character, I hung my head, and my shoulders slumped. "I'm really sorry."

"I know you 'really' are. But you know what's going to happen, don't you?"

"Yes."

"Yes?"

"Yes, sir."

"That's better." He walked into the dining room and sat down on an armless side chair. "Now," he said, drumming his fingers on the wooden tabletop, "what shall it be tonight?"

I knew exactly what he was referring to. How did I want my spanking? I considered the wooden ruler, the Ping-Pong paddle and the wooden spoon we keep in a drawer in the bedroom. I could almost feel the slap against my buttocks. "Please," I said. deciding, exaggerating the shaking of my voice, "not the ruler."

I could barely control my legs as he said, "Of course. The ruler. Get it for me."

"Oh, please, sir, anything but that."

He merely raised an eyebrow, and I scurried into the bedroom and quickly returned with the ruler. The feel of it in my hand made my ass tingle and my pussy flow. I handed it to him and dropped my gaze. "That's a good girl," he said. "Now remove your bra and panties, but leave the rest of your clothes on."

I started to turn away, but he snapped, "I want to watch."

Slowly I turned and faced him, button by button opening my shirt. I do love to tease him, you know. Then I slipped it off, quickly removed my bra and pulled the shirt back on, leaving it open down the front.

"Panties," he said.

Had I suspected that we would play? Was that why I chose to wear a skirt to work that day? I reached beneath the soft flowing cotton and pulled down my panties. Now beneath my skirt I wore only a garter belt and stockings. I never wear panty hose anymore. Gary smiled at me and spread his knees, then crooked his finger at me. I slowly walked between his legs.

"You were a bad girl," he said, reaching up and pinching one nipple hard enough to make me wince.

"Yes, sir," I said, so hot now I thought I could come without his ever touching me.

"You know what happens now, don't you?" He pinched the other nipple.

"Yes, sir."

Now he grabbed a nipple in each hand and twisted until I gasped. Then he pushed his chair away from the table and patted his lap with the ruler. "But, sir," I said, trembling.

"No buts, my love." He continued to pat his thighs with the erotic strip of wood. "Right here, right now."

I could barely make my body cooperate as I slowly stretched across his lap, my tits suspended on one side, my legs hanging on the other. He reached down and pulled my skirt up so my bare butt was exposed. Then he stroked the ruler across my cheeks, the cool of the wood on my hot skin. His other hand reached into my shirt and tugged on my hanging nipple. "Are you ready?"

I sighed and said, "Yes, sir."

The first slap was soft, almost gentle, the next few a bit harder. "How many do you suppose you deserve for your little spending spree?" he asked.

"Maybe five," I said, knowing we'd already done four.

His chuckle was warm. "Not a chance, my love. Maybe fifteen tonight." He stopped pulling on my breast and transferred the ruler to his other hand. Then he reached between my legs and fingered my pussy. "You're so wet, love. I'll bet you could come for the first time right now." With that word, he pressed against my clit, and I came. I hadn't realized how close I was, but the spasms rocked through me immediately. As I came down, he said, "That's better. Now that the edge is off, we can get down to business."

My juices were now flooding down the insides of my thighs, but he was right. The edge was off just enough for me to enjoy the pleasure/pain of the next several slaps. Slowly, as my ass heated and began to burn, the heat transferred to my crotch, and I rose toward another orgasm.

"That's ten," Gary said, "but let's hold off on the rest for right now." He pushed me off his lap and unzipped his fly. His cock sprang free through the opening in his shorts, as big as I had ever seen it. "Give me your tits."

I knelt between his thighs and took his cock between my breasts, using his precome to wet the valley. He closed his eyes and thrust between my tits as I flicked my tongue across the tip each time I could reach it. Like me earlier, he couldn't wait, and it took only a few moments until thick semen spurted. I licked him clean, and soon I was across his lap, feeling the final five slaps of the ruler across my already-sore butt.

By then he was hard again, as I knew this game would make him, and I quickly climbed on his lap, facing him, and inserted his cock into my hot pussy. He pulled back and rubbed his wet cock over my hot bottom, then rammed himself back in. Straddling his lap, I levered myself up and down, my head thrown back, his mouth on my nipple. With a roar, he came again, and I quickly followed.

I think we must have dozed, still tangled on the chair. Eventually I stood up and used my panties and shirttails to wipe the juices from my legs and crotch. "God, that was fabulous," Gary said, slowly standing up and draping an arm over my shoulders.

"Wonderful," I said, my bottom sore and my pussy satisfied. "Maybe soon you'll do something naughty."

Gary's eye lit up. "I might just do that."

# My Little Secret

I'm a sun worshipper. I know all about skin cancer and all that bad stuff I'm supposed to be worried about, but I love the feel of the sun on my skin so much that I just ignore the rest. My husband and I bought a house in the suburbs recently, and the most wonderful thing about it is the backyard. I quickly discovered that I can lie out on my lounge chair in my bikini and get as much sun as I want. It's so fabulous.

One Saturday afternoon, I had dozed off in the yard while my husband, Jim, was off playing tennis with some of his buddies. I had slathered my body with number-four sun stuff to keep my skin moist and smooth, and just basked. At about four, I heard Jim at the back door. "Hi, love," I called lazily. "How come you're home so early?"

"Pete twisted his ankle and went home, so here I am."

"Is he okay?"

"Oh, yeah. Nothing serious. He just wanted to rest."

"Wanna join me?" I asked, not eager to give up my last hour of sun.

"Be right out," he called. He returned about five minutes later in his cute little black Speedo. He's really got a great body from all that tennis and stuff. He pulled a lounge chair up beside mine, slathered his body with my number-four and stretched out. "You know, this really feels great," he said. "I can understand why you like it. But why do you wear a bathing suit?"

"Why?"

"Sure. No one can see you at this end of the yard."

I looked around and saw that Jim was right. This corner was pretty secluded, protected by some trees and a large hedge. "I think it would feel really strange, even if I knew no one could watch."

Jim stood up and pulled off his Speedo. "I think it would feel really decadent." Naked, his cock at sort of half-mast, he stretched out on the chair again on his back. "God, this really does feel great. Sun on parts of me that have never had sun before. You've got to try this."

I pondered, then realized that he was right. I've always wanted to sunbathe nude, but I've never had the opportunity. I sat up and removed my top, feeling the sun on my breasts for the first time. Jim looked at me and grinned. "You're skin is so white, you need to be careful about sunburn."

"It's after four, so I don't think I'm in much danger."

"Let me put some sun stuff on you anyway. I've got some number-fifteen in the house." He disappeared and came back with a large bottle. I reached for it, but he playfully slapped my hand. "I'll do it."

He poured out a palmful of the stuff and rubbed his hands together. Then, as I sat on my chair, he filled his hands with my breasts, slathering the lotion over my hot skin. He alternately kneaded and swirled his fingers softly, exciting me, as I'm sure he knew he would. "You better stop that," I said. "I want some sun, not to stage a show for the neighbors."

"I love the way your body shines from all that oil you put on," he said, running his palms over my ribs.

I laughed as he tickled my sides, then slid his fingers over my thighs. "You know, you can take this off too," he said, pulling at the ties at the sides of my bikini bottom.

Scandalized but intrigued and very excited, I thought, What the heck, and untied the bottom and pulled it off. "Spread your legs," Jim said. "If the sun on your pussy feels anything like the sun on my cock, it will be quite a sensation." He stretched me out on the chair and arranged me so the sun shone on my groin. Then he pulled my legs apart so my inner lips felt the heat. Shit, it was the sexiest feeling I've had in a long time. Heat made my pussy almost glow. I was soaked from the excitement of it all, and I could feel my pussy twitch and my tissues swell. "I knew it would blow you away," Jim said, and I realized that he was still sitting at the foot of my chair, staring at the private area between my legs.

Now I won't say that he's never seen me before, but not like this, in the sun, in the open air. It was sort of deliciously embarrassing, if that's possible. And it only aroused me more. "I think you need more sun goo," he said, as he poured another handful.

I was unable to speak, so hot and so hungry I wanted to grab Jim and jump his cock. But I didn't, allowing the excitement to build. Then I felt his fingers on the insides of my thighs, slowly spreading sun oil all over. He delved into all my folds, rubbing my clit, until I thought I would die from it. Not yet.

I sat up and grabbed the bottle of number-fifteen. "You're in as much danger as I am," I said. "Your cock and balls have never been in the sun either." How I managed that full thought I'll never know, but from his leer, Jim heard me loud and clear. He moved back to his chair and lay back, his cock now fully erect, sticking straight up from its nest of black hair. I filled my palm with the lotion, then wrapped my hand around his erection and slowly spread the stuff from base to tip. Let me assure you, I know exactly what he likes, so I gave him the best hand job I could, keeping him just on the edge but not letting him come. I rubbed lotion on his balls, and when I smoothed some on the insides of his ass cheeks right up to his anus, I thought I'd lost him.

It was almost too late, but I straddled his cock and slid my oily body down onto him. I leaned forward, rubbing my slick breasts against his hairy chest. He grabbed my ass cheeks, and raised and lowered my body until I was sure he would come. Then, as he was about to climax, he sat me up and slipped his hand between us so he could rub my clit.

We don't usually try for simultaneous orgasms, since to do that, someone's always rushing while the other's waiting, but this afternoon, in the sunshine, we came together, me with a groan and Jim with his usual bellow.

I think we must have dozed for a little while, with me still on top of him, his cock slowly softening inside me. Finally we separated, and weak-kneed, I moved to my lounger. It was then that I noticed a small space in the hedge and saw our neighbor Matt's back as he followed his wife into his house from his backyard. Had they been watching? Had they heard our lovemaking? I opened my mouth to tell Jim, but then I stopped. I loved making love in the sunshine, and although Jim's no prude—he was the one who convinced me to take off my suit, after all—I don't think he'd be willing to do it again if he thought anyone could see. So, I think, for now it will remain my little secret.

# No Ticket for Me!

There were no markings on the car that pulled her over at ten o'clock one Tuesday evening, but Sue knew that the man who climbed out would be in uniform. "I wasn't speeding," she explained as the man strode to her driver's side window. "I know I wasn't. I never speed. Well, almost never." Stop babbling, she told herself. You're talking from nervousness.

"May I see your license and registration?" the officer said.

As she leaned over to fetch her purse, she said, "Isn't there any way we can work this out? I've had a few tickets recently, and I'd love to make this go away."

"No way, lady," the cop said. "You were doing almost forty in a twenty-five."

As she handed him her license and registration, she looked him over. About six feet tall, with soft brown eyes and a thick moustache over a really sexy mouth. Good hands, with short, well-trimmed nails, she thought, as he took the documents. Sexy hands. "Are you sure?" she said.

"I could let you go with a warning," he said, then paused, "if you cooperate."

Cooperate. She knew what was coming. Was she willing

to go through with it just to avoid a ticket? She became aware of her sweaty palms and trembling fingers. "What would I have to do?" she asked, not totally sure she wanted to avoid a ticket quite this much.

He raised a thick eyebrow, and his eyes roamed over as much of her as he could see. "Get out," he snapped.

She climbed out of the car, and he grabbed her arm and pulled her around to the front so the headlights illuminated her. She wasn't bad looking for a forty-year-old mother of three. She kept herself pretty trim and didn't look too bad in her jeans and sweater. She stood up straight and tried to tempt him into overlooking her ticket.

"Not bad," he said. "You live around here?"

"J-j-just down the block," she said.

He looked at the two small cards in his hand. "Husband home?"

"Not 'til much later."

"Okay. Drive home very slowly, and I'll meet you there. My shift just ended."

Sue made her way to her house, pulled the car into her garage and waited, hoping the cop wouldn't follow. He did, his unmarked car pulling into the driveway behind her. He walked into the garage and pressed the button to lower the door.

There was a streetlight right at the end of the driveway, so there was some illumination coming in through the small windows as Sue got out of her car. "Get your sweater off," he said. "Bra too. I want to see what I'm risking my career for."

Shit, Sue thought. She looked him over, trying to concentrate on the sexy things about him. And she did love a strong, masterful male. She pulled her sweater off over her head and tossed it into the front seat, her bra following quickly.

The cop reached out and grabbed her breast, squeezing hard, then pinched her nipple. It was partly humiliating, partly very erotic. "Nice tits," he said. "You going to cooperate fully?"

"Y-y-yes."

"Not good enough," he said, pulling his handcuffs from his belt. He pulled her arms behind her and locked her wrists together. "The bedroom," he said.

He opened the door from the garage into the house, and Sue led the way upstairs to the bedroom. Slowly, as she watched, he removed his jacket and shirt. "Come here." As she approached, his arm snaked behind her and dragged her naked breasts against his hairy chest. He moved back and forth, rubbing her nipples against his skin, the sensation scary but erotic. Without a word, he pressed his mouth against hers, his kiss hot and demanding. When her mouth didn't open immediately, he pressed his tongue against her lips, forcing her to admit him.

The kiss went on for a long time, until his breathing was rapid and hers shaky. He grabbed the back of her shoulder-length hair and pulled her head back so his mouth could rake along her throat and across to her shoulder. He leaned over and took one now-erect nipple between his teeth and bit, hard enough to make her jump.

"Over here," he said, almost dragging her to the bed. He unlocked one wrist and then looped the free cuff around the bedpost and loudly snapped it shut. He then pushed her down until she was lying on the bedspread, fastened to the headboard, one arm over her head. "Now that's what I call a cooperative woman."

With efficient motions, he removed the rest of his clothing and hers, then pushed her feet up until her heels were against her buttocks, her knees spread, her pussy wide open for his inspection. "Nice cunt, lady," he growled. He stretched out, his head between her thighs, and peered at her private parts. She trembled, both with fear and with a reluctant excitement. She hated how easily she'd become aroused. Then he explored her wet, swollen flesh, running his fingers over every part of her. "You're very wet. I guess you like this sort of thing."

"Not a chance," she said, knowing she was lying.

He chuckled. "Your body tells a different story. He slid a finger slowly into her, meeting no resistance as he entered. She reached down with her free hand to push him away, but he slapped her hand aside. "Cooperation," he said, and she let her hand fall to her side.

Then the thrusting began. In an imitation of lovemaking, he entered and withdrew, his finger soon joined by a second and then a third. She couldn't keep her hips still, and she rose to meet each thrust. "This is wrong," she said.

"Yeah, but so hot."

When she was about to climax, he crawled up her body and rammed his erection into her, driving his cock deep. Over and over he pounded, until she climaxed, bright primary colors echoing behind her eyes, unable to contain her screams. Moments later, he came deep inside her.

Without another word, they dozed, then he removed the handcuff and stretched out beside her. "That was wonderful."

"God, yes," she said. "Best yet. I'll just brush my teeth, then we can get some sleep. We've got to pick the kids up before nine. Mom and Dad have a lot to do tomorrow."

"Don't bring me back to reality just yet," Sue's husband said. "I like it here. So just cooperate lady, and we'll see what happens next."

# Outside My Window

Ididn't mean to watch, but who can help it when something so yummy is going on? They were doing it, in their bedroom, with the shade up and the window wide open. Okay, so I shouldn't have been watching, but it was so hot—both temperature hot and sexy hot.

It all started when, on a day I had taken off from work to run a batch of errands I never got a chance to do otherwise, I walked by my bedroom window and glanced out. It was three in the afternoon, and there they were, naked, making out like crazy. He was on top and had his hands on her tits. I could almost feel them on mine, kneading, squeezing, pulling at the nipples. I'll admit it right now. It made me hot. I considered just pulling down my jeans and rubbing myself, but I decided to wait. Anticipation is always wonderful and makes it even better in the end.

Finally the woman slid around, then down in the bed, and took his hard cock in her mouth while he buried his face in her crotch. I was viewing a really good sixty-nine, and I could almost feel his staff in my throat. I licked my lips, then I crouched, propped my elbows on the windowsill and rested my chin on my hands to keep myself from stroking my pussy, as I enjoyed seeing her giving head, her long hair hanging over the end of the bed. As he thrust into her mouth, I could see his butt muscles—he had a great butt—clench and relax.

"What's so fascinating?" my boyfriend, Chuck, asked from behind me.

I must have jumped three feet, and I almost hit my head on the window frame. "What the heck are you doing home?"

"Got off early. The big guys arrived, and they shut everything down while they conduct their annual inspection. What are you watching?"

For some reason, I didn't want him to know what I was watching, so I moved away from the window and grabbed him around the waist. "Nothing, just daydreaming. About your sexy body actually."

"You're sounding very guilty, Patty. I wonder what you were watching." He easily moved me aside and went to the window. Meekly I followed. They were still doing it. Now he was on the bottom, with the woman straddling him, bouncing up and down, her head thrown back. It was a scene straight out of a porno video. "You were watching them fuck," he said, his voice stern. "That's a very naughty thing to do."

"I'm sorry. I guess it was, but I just couldn't help it. And they don't seem to mind."

"I mind."

"Why the hell do you mind what I watch out the window?"

"Because it's up to me to make you understand what's nice and what's not."

"Bullshit!" What right did he have to decide what I could and couldn't do. My sexy mood evaporated as my anger rose.

As I got madder, he got calmer. "You're being a very bad girl. You need to be punished."

"Bullshit!" I said again.

He just smiled an infuriating smile, grabbed my wrist and dragged me to our bed. He sat on the edge and pulled me down across his lap. "Very bad girl," he said, slapping my upturned butt.

Through my jeans, his swats really didn't hurt, but the indignity of it all was too much. "Cut that out!" Actually, I do love it when Chuck gets aggressive, and he knows it.

"You. Were. Very. Bad." He punctuated his words with slaps on my ass.

We've never played this way before, but I found that my anger quickly dissipated, replaced by a delicious warmth in my crotch. I decided to play along. I knew he'd never hurt me, and I'd read a lot about dominant/submissive games. "I was not," I said, snapping out the words.

"You were, and you need to be punished for it." He pushed me off his lap, and I landed in a heap on the floor. "Remove those jeans. You'll never learn anything with all that padding."

I had a decision to make. I could stop the whole thing with just the word "stop." He'd know that I meant it, and I had no doubt that he'd stop. Or I could run away, let him chase me until he caught me, and we could make lovely love in the middle of the afternoon. Or . . . "Yes, sir," I said.

"That's a good girl," he said, his voice ominous.

I pulled off my jeans and looked at him questioningly. "Your panties can stay on for now," he said. "Wait here."

He rummaged in the closet until he found our toy bag, then brought it back to the bed and dumped the contents within easy reach. "Assume the position," he said. I lay across his thighs, still dressed in my shirt, socks, bra and panties. "Now let's see where we are." He pulled the crotch of my panties aside and ran his finger through my wetness. "Nice and juicy," he said. Then I felt a dildo pressed against my opening and pushed inside. No sexy rubbing or thrusting, just a businesslike push and it was in. Then Chuck pulled the panties back so the fabric was holding the dildo in place.

"What the . . . ?"

"No talking," he barked.

I slammed my mouth shut.

"Good. Now, I think five for starters." We had a small paddle in the toy bag, bought several months before, when we were thinking about trying something like this, but we'd never used it. He used it now. "One," he said, and the paddle landed on one butt cheek. It wasn't quite painful, but it certainly must have reddened my ass. It also moved the dildo slightly.

"Two." The paddle landed on the other cheek. "Three." It was getting more and more painful—well, sore, really. He seemed to know just how hard to hit to make it sting but not to hurt me so badly that I'd want him to stop. "Four." Amazingly enough, every slap made me hotter. "Five." I was ready to come right then.

"How are you doing, naughty girl?"

"I'm fine," I said, hissing the words through my clenched teeth.

I felt him move and then pull aside the panties again. Another dildo. He rubbed it through my soaking pussy, around the first one, then around my rear hole. We'd teased with anal sex occasionally, up to but not including actual penis penetration. Well, it wasn't his penis, but the dildo that penetrated my ass. "Don't come," he said, his tone harsh, "or you'll have to be punished again."

"Don't come?" I choked out. "You're making me come."

"Too bad. If you come, I'll spank you again."

It was torture of a wonderful kind. He played with the two dildos, pulling and pushing, tapping the ends, until I thought I'd burst. I bit the inside of my lip and clenched my thighs to try not to climax. Let me tell you, it wasn't easy.

By now, Chuck was hot as well. He eased me onto the floor, on my knees between his legs, and took out his cock. "Suck me off. If you do it well, I might let you come."

I'm very good. I took him deep, then pulled back, licking the tip with the flat of my tongue the way he likes. Deep, lick, deep, lick. By then, he was having a difficult time not coming himself. "Don't come," I said, slipping out of my subservient role. "Don't you dare."

We moved onto the bed, sixty-nine, like the couple in the window, me on top with Chuck's cock in my mouth, him on the bottom playing with the dildos through my panties. It was difficult to concentrate on my mouth while he played with my pussy. Then I felt him start to jerk, and I knew he was close. Only seconds later, my mouth was filled with his semen, and I let myself come, rockets of pleasure racing through my body.

We ended up cuddled together, both of us almost fully dressed, with the dildos still in place. "God," Chuck said. "Fabulous."

"Me too," I said.

He reached down and wriggled his hand into my crotch, playing with the vaginal dildo. "Again?"

I rolled over on my back. "Why not?"

Please turn the page for an exciting sneak peek of
Joan Elizabeth Lloyd's next new novel,
HOT SUMMER NIGHTS

# *Chapter 1*

Burned out, Leslie thought. What a ridiculous concept. She loved her job—most of the time—and was phenomenally well paid for it. Plus, everyone who did business with her told her how wonderful and talented she was. How could she be burned out? Well, she sighed, as she drove east through Connecticut on Route 95, maybe this vacation would help her sort through her feelings. She wasn't about to give up her job, and yet, she wasn't looking forward to her eventual return to business either.

When had she started thinking burnout?

It had begun several weeks ago, with a favorite client, Bob Rowan. She had been using the motel room in Club Fantasy, a simple room that could be rearranged to become a photo studio, the master suite of a mansion or, as it had been that evening, a simple bedroom in a simple house in the suburbs. That evening, dressed in a sheer, peach-colored nightgown and red silk robe, she had been sitting at the dressing table, brushing her hair, when she heard someone in the closet. Heart speeding, as it always did when something like the action of that evening began, she kept taking long strokes through her shoulder-length ash blonde hair and glanced into the mirror at the door to the closet, where she knew Bob was hiding.

They'd played this fantasy so many times that she knew exactly what was going to happen, but still she threw herself into her role and played innocent. As the closet door slowly opened, she whipped around. "What's that . . . ?"

Despite the warm, early summer weather outside, Bob was dressed in a black turtleneck, black jeans, black socks and tennis shoes. Black leather gloves covered his hands, and a black watch cap hid his salt-and-pepper crew cut. "Say nothing, do nothing, and everything will be fine," he growled.

"What the hell are you doing here? Get out of my house!" She spoke softly yet forcefully.

"I'm here for you," Bob said. In only two strides, he was behind her, holding her hair twisted in his fist, pulling her head back.

"You're hurting me," she said, knowing that the slight pain he caused was all part of this playlet and helped keep her in character.

"Only a little," he said, a slight grin causing creases to form around his deep brown eyes.

She remained silent, although she could have screamed or protested. She knew he wouldn't stop unless she used the safe word they'd agreed on.

He pulled harder, forcing her to stand to ease the pressure on her scalp. "I didn't think you'd be home so early," he said.

"I'm sure you didn't," she said, her eyes narrowing, her pulse pounding.

"But you know," he continued, "this might be an added bonus. I get to steal your jewels and have you too."

"My jewelry. Of course. Listen," she said, sounding as

reasonable as she could, "take my jewels, but then just leave. I promise I won't tell anyone."

"I know you won't tell anyone, and we're going to have some fun together before I leave." He dragged her toward the bed and tossed her onto it, throwing her robe open, revealing her peach-colored satin nightgown beneath. His eyes roamed her body, as if he'd never seen it before. "Lovely. Truly lovely."

Her eyes widened. "What are you going to do?"

His laugh was genuine. "As if you didn't know."

It was so theatrical, but in its own way, delicious too. It was all she could do not to giggle. She sighed, heaving her ample bosom, pulling herself back into character. Tightening her grip on herself, she said, "Please. Don't hurt me."

Bob opened the bedside table drawer and pulled out several strips of fabric lined with soft fur; she'd put them there for him. With little fuss despite her struggles, he tied Leslie's wrists to the bedposts, the bindings secure, and pulled just tight enough to stretch her arms wide without undue discomfort.

She kicked and twisted, careful not to injure him or herself, yet with ease, he grabbed one ankle and fastened a strip around it, then attached it to one of the bed legs. Then he made quick work of the other. Leslie was always surprised at how hot it all made her, despite the fact that she was playing a part. She was wet, her nipples tight, her belly throbbing. Bob ran a gloved finger through her folds and laughed. "This really turns you on, doesn't it?"

"Yes," she answered, both for her character and for herself.

"Good. I'm glad." He grabbed the front of her gown and pulled, ripping it easily along seams that had been carefully loosened. "Because you're mine, and I intend to take you. Slowly."

"Please," she whimpered, "don't. I don't want you."

"Your body says different," Bob said, rubbing his dampened fingers together. "I hope you're not going to scream. If you do, I'll have to gag you too."

She shook her head violently. "I'll be quiet."

He cupped her chin and leaned over, pressing his mouth against hers, his tongue pushing its way into her cavern. Leslie loved the way he kissed, molding his lips against hers, drawing out all the pleasures within her. She felt her body relaxing, but that wasn't the way the fantasy was supposed to play out. She jerked herself back into character, twisting her head. "Don't do that!"

He raised an eyebrow, and his smile was sardonic. "I'll do anything I please. After all, you're in no position to argue." He knelt beside the bed and took one erect nipple in his mouth while he pinched the other between his fingers. She arched her back and gasped at the sudden onslaught. God, she loved what he did to her body every time they acted out this fantasy.

Finally, after what seemed like hours of playing with her breasts, he stood and removed his clothing, leaving his butter-soft leather gloves on. Several months ago, he'd added them to his attire, and later he'd said how much that increased his pleasure. Leslie didn't know why, nor did she care. The important thing was that he enjoy himself to the utmost. She looked at him, slightly paunchy, with heavy thighs and a chest covered with whorls of straight hair. She was delighted to see that his erection was full and hard.

He grabbed her hair and twisted her face to the side, and, knowing his next move, she opened her mouth so he could ram his engorged cock into it. "Be a good little girl," he said, "and suck me good."

She did, using everything she knew about the way he

liked it. She flicked the tip with her tongue, then licked the length of him as he dictated the rhythm. She sucked and lapped at him, until she knew he was close. She wanted to fondle him, but her hands were still tied, so she used her mouth to bring him closer and closer to orgasm.

Finally she heard the deep catch in his breath, and he spurted into her mouth. She swallowed as fast as she could, milking the last of his orgasm from him. When he was fully satisfied, he untied one of her wrists and dropped into a chair to catch his breath. "Satisfy yourself while I watch," he snapped, and she quickly moved her hand to her crotch, easily finding her erect clit and rubbing. His eyes were fixed on her fingers as she pleasured herself. His actions had so aroused her that it took only moments for her to climax, a small moan the only sign.

Minutes later, he untied the remaining restraints and quickly put on his clothing. "That was wonderful, as always. By the way, I'll be away for August, but I'll call and make an appointment for September."

She slowly sat up. "I'll look forward to it." That was when it had first hit her. Would she look forward to it? Although the sex was satisfying, and, of the fifteen hundred dollar charge to his credit card, a thousand of it would find its way into her bank account, she was restless, bored, tired of all the things she had to do to maintain herself as one of the highest paid "entertainers" in Manhattan.

It was almost midnight, and she knew she was the only one left upstairs in the brownstone that housed Club Fantasy, one of the most exclusive and well-attended brothels in the city. So after Bob was gone, she crossed to the bathroom, gloriously naked except for the wide-open robe, clutching the torn nightgown to keep from tripping. She knew the club's bodyguard was downstairs, closing up, but he wouldn't disturb her. "Good night, Rock," she called, and after a moment, heard his answering, "Good night, Leslie. I'll leave the alarm off, so set it when you go."

"Will do." She heard his door close as she stripped off her robe and tossed the shreds of her nightgown into the trash. *Just part of the expense of doing business*, she thought, as she turned on the hot water in the shower.

Bob would be away for August. How delightful. Quite a few of her regular clients would also be gone, so August should prove to be a very quiet month. *God*, she thought, *I could use some quiet.* Some peace and quiet. Suddenly, as she stood beneath the spray and soaped her tired body, she realized that she wanted—no, desperately needed—some time away.

Was she suffering from burnout? Who cared what name you called it? In a flash of understanding, she realized that she hadn't enjoyed her job in months. Yes, she got sexual pleasure out of her encounters, and emotional pleasure out of pleasing her clients, but where was the fun, the adventure, the newness, of satisfying a client for the first time, of watching his, or even her, face as they found something they had so long sought? It had been so great in the beginning; now it was just routine. Where had that explosive fire gone?

As the days passed, Leslie realized that, as exciting as the fantasy games were for her clients, they had all become boring for her. Boring. Great sex with rich and powerful men had become almost tedious. She'd been able to satisfy all her clients, but she knew that it was only a matter of time before they'd start to become bored with her. And that must never happen.

She'd been working for the owners of Club Fantasy, where dreams were fulfilled for a hefty fee, for almost nine years. She worked five evenings a week and frequently made several thousand dollars each night. She played roles as varied as a harem dancer, a maid captured by a pirate, a prison guard and a young teenaged girl. She also had dinner with movers and shakers, with hanky panky afterward. It was wonderful fun, but it was also lots of work. In order to be able to converse with them, she read the *New York Times* every day, and *People*, a news weekly and at least one sports magazine each week.

She wasn't ashamed of what she did at all. She entertained, gave pleasure, and was well paid for it. She saw nothing immoral about any of it. Illegal? Possibly, but the New York City police left her and Club Fantasy alone. Maybe that was because the owners of the club knew a little more about some government officials than those officials wanted publicized. And the clients were thoroughly vetted as well. For whatever reason, she felt no compunctions about what she did.

As she drove through the early August heat, Leslie thought about it all. She hadn't had a truly filling meal except with a client since she had put on several pounds while cruising on a yacht with a wealthy stockbroker the previous winter. One of her regulars had actually mentioned that she looked a little "softer," as he'd put it. Since then, dieting had become a way of life, as had weekly trips to the hairstylist and the nail salon.

So, several weeks before, she'd called a real estate agency that specialized in vacation rentals. "It's already mid-July, Ms. Morgan," a motherly woman named Janice had said. "It's going to be really tough to find something for August, but we do occasionally have cancellations. Let me see what I can come up with."

A few days later, the agent had called back, suggesting the cottage in Sound's End, Connecticut, right on the water. "The guy who rented it had a minor family emergency.

Actually, his youngest broke her leg in a bicycle accident. Anyway, he's cancelling out on this lovely little place he rented for August. It's really part of a hotel, but it's a free-standing house, one of several they own adjacent to the main building, and it's got all the amenities. They treat it like any other room—maid service and such—but it's more private. There's a full kitchen, if you want to cook, and if not, there's a dining room at the hotel. You can have it for the entire month of August and through Labor Day, if you like. My client will be delighted to have his deposit back." She mentioned a substantial price, but it had taken Leslie only a moment's thought. Salt air, relaxing all day and sleeping alone each night. It had sounded like heaven. "Done." And now she was on her way there.

She'd memorized the directions and now took the exit east of Old Saybrook, and drove toward the tiny town of Sound's End, so named, she'd learned when she looked the town up on the Internet, because it was located directly opposite the eastern-most tip of Long Island, so was technically at the intersection of the Long Island Sound and the Atlantic Ocean. As she slowed to thirty miles per hour, she looked around. The town appeared to be a typical New England town, with white buildings and a large town square with a veterans' memorial basking in afternoon sunshine. There were three banks, a couple of gas stations, a post office and a row of small, one-story, boutiquey stores, including two that sold tee shirts and other tourist items, one that seemed to specialize in photography and one that had a for-lease sign in the window. The main shopping area, on the other side of the main street, consisted of a florist, a small market and a ladies' clothing shop. Interspersed were several restaurants: a diner, an American-style family restaurant specializing in seafood called the Wayfarer, a Chinese sit-down place and one that specialized in take-out, an

Italian restaurant called Victorio's and a pizzeria. *I guess I'm not the only one who doesn't cook*, Leslie thought. Since it was midafternoon, most were now closed.

She stopped at the small market. A sign over the door read "Martinelli's Market—Italian Specialties," and she climbed out of the car. The air here in Sound's End was completely different from what she'd left in New York City. Here it was a bit cooler, but the sun was intense and there was a hint of salt in the air. She inhaled deeply, then turned her face to the sun and stood there, listening to the sounds of kids running around the play area in the little park between the library and the market. She couldn't control the wide grin that split her face.

The market looked unimpressive from the outside, but inside it was filled with unusual Italian delicacies. One case was filled with sausage, much of it homemade. She read a few labels: veal and Parmesan; pork, oregano and mozzarella; sweet sausage with dill. She pushed her cart toward another glass-fronted display case filled with delicatessen goodies: meats and cheeses of all kinds, homemade salads and antipasti. This small, unassuming market would put even her Korean grocery to shame.

She spent almost an hour filling her shopping cart with the things she'd need for at least a couple of days. Since she seldom ate at home anyway, she kept little in her Manhattan apartment, so buying food was an adventure. She poked around, lifting cans and reading the ingredients lists and nutritional labels, selecting those with low saturated fat, sugar and calories. Then, with a little thrill and a shrug, she threw several fattening, totally-bad-for-her items in her cart. Grinning over a jar of chunky peanut butter, a can of pork and beans, another of ravioli and a third of deviled ham, she headed for the checkout counter. She'd have to investigate the goodies in the cases another day. She considered that she might actually try cooking somewhere along the line, but for now, she'd just open cans. Cooking. That's a good idea. Something totally out of character for her. Maybe she'd surf the Web and find recipes she could actually make. According to the agent, the house came with a fully equipped kitchen. Cooking. What a concept.

As she unloaded her purchases, she actually felt herself unwind. With a deep sigh, she watched a middle-aged man check the prices on the cans and boxes, and ring up the items on an old-fashioned cash register. "Welcome to the neighborhood," he said, his voice light and cheery, with a slight New England twang. After her equally cheerful thanks, he continued, "You're new here. Going to be here for a while?"

"Yeah. I'm here until Labor Day, and I am really looking forward to it."

"Where are you staying?" he asked as he rang up her jar of peanut butter.

"Someplace called the Rogers Cottage. It's part of the Atlantic Beach Hotel."

The man put the jar down and reached out a large hand. "We'll be neighbors," he said. "My wife, the kids and I live just across the street. I'm Joe Martinelli, and my wife's Marie. Welcome to the neighborhood."

Well, this certainly wasn't New York City. "I'm Leslie Morgan." She took his hand and enjoyed his firm grip. It was novel for a man to be friendly to her without wanting any part of her body. Leslie knew she was attractive, and she'd been told that she seemed to exude an air of sensuality from every pore. This "friendly thing" was really nice. "Nice to meet you."

"Listen," Joe said, picking up a loaf of whole-grain bread and checking the price, "we have a cookout the first Friday of each month, right beside the beach. It will be kind of in your side yard. I want you to be sure to come, and bring your appetite."

Tomorrow evening. It was a temptation. Being around real people, just because. No one to impress. But . . . "Thanks for the invitation, but I couldn't impose."

"It's no imposition. Marie loves to cook. We always have lots of folks from the houses around, so one more person won't even make a dent. And, of course, you'll get to meet all the neighbors." He chuckled. "Actually, you'll already have met Suze. She makes sure to get all the dope on all the new folks. Quickly and efficiently."

"Suze?"

"It's really Susan Murdock, but no one's called her Susan in forever. It's just Suze. She's the mayor of Sound's End, and she feels that she has to know everything about everyone. She's up for reelection in the fall this year, and now she also campaigns all the time. Although you can't vote, you might have the opportunity to influence someone who does, so she'll be all over you." He sighed. "She means well, though. Anyway, we'd love to have you. If it would make you feel better, you can bring something to eat, or put a ten-dollar bill in the coffee can on the grill to cover expenses. I'll look forward to seeing you there."

It sounded so comfortable that Leslie knew she wouldn't be able to resist, and making a contribution would make it feel less like an imposition. "I'd love to."

Joe grabbed a sheet of paper from beside the register. "You'll need a tide table. Lots of what goes on here depends on the tides." He stuffed it into one of her plastic bags. "Do you have sunblock?" Joe added.

"I've got a tube of number forty-five in my car."

"Good, use it. Sorry. There I go sounding like your father."

Leslie winked. "You're not nearly old enough to be my father, and anyway, my father never treated me this well."

"Okay, older brother."

Her grin widening still further, she winked and said, "Agreed, bro."

As Leslie paid for her groceries, she felt herself relax still more. She hadn't even seen her cottage yet, and already she'd made a friend in the neighborhood. She hadn't realized how uneasy this trip had made her. It had seemed like such a good idea when she made her plans, but she was a city girl at heart. What would she find to do for a month in a small beach community with rural people and no subways? Now she felt a bit better. This would be just what she needed.

Dear Reader,

I hope you've enjoyed the tales I've shared with you here, and I also hope that your bedroom life is better for having read at least one of them. You might wonder which is my personal favorite. When I write one, it's my favorite, but when I create the next, that one takes its place. Therefore, I'd love to know which ones in particular you liked, so I can write similar ones for my next collection. I used several readers' suggestions for the stories here. Drop me an e-mail at Joan@JoanELLoyd.com or a snail-mail at P.O. Box 221, Yorktown Heights, New York 10598.

I also invite you to visit my Web site at www.JoanELLoyd. com. I post a new short story every other month or so, ones I know you'll enjoy, as you did these. Drop me a line and let me know what you think of my tales.

*Joan Lloyd*